THE BRAINWAVE

THE BRAINWAVE

Evon Schuller

The Book Guild Ltd.
Sussex, England

*To Brenda Joyce and June Headford with
heartfelt gratitude for their patience
and encouragement.*

The Book Guild Limited
Temple House
25 High Street
Lewes, Sussex

First published 1992
© Evon Schuller 1991

Set in Baskerville

Typesetting by Dataset
St Leonards-on-Sea, East Sussex

Printed in Great Britain by
Billings and Sons Ltd
Worcester

British Library Cataloguing in Publication Data

Schuller, Evon
The brainwave
I. Title
823. 914 [F]

ISBN 0 86332 635 8

1

The year was 1994. Having miraculously escaped a nuclear holocaust, the people of planet Earth were in even more danger. Apart from polluted water and chemical plants spewing their toxic waste into the now almost unbreathable air, the earth had tilted on its axis and was revolving faster. This had caused the pace of life to increase and people were cracking up daily. Weather conditions had changed, bringing famine to areas which had been plentiful and grain and growth to the parched deserts of North Africa and Arabia.

Many people had given up their homes and left everything, taking only a suitcase of clothes. There was no petrol so they had to walk, except those who had bicycles or maybe a horse.

One such family were the Bakers. Don Baker had been a successful accountant; his wife Nora was a beautician and their one son, Robert, aged thirteen, attended the junior section of the Scientific Experimental College. They had a smart detached house with a garage where an old Jaguar and a Mini were mouldering away. The garden had once been a joy to see with its sweeping lawn, flower beds, fruit trees and, at the bottom, a vegetable patch. Now, even though it was only the middle of August, the grass looked more like sand, the flowers were sparse and droopy and the leaves on the apple and pear trees were already brown and crackly.

The door opened and Nora went round to the garage. As she did so, Mary Gruber came out of the house next door. Most of the houses in Eland Road were of the same style – the only difference being what was inside. Mary Gruber had always admired the Baker house as everything there was of the best and always neat and tidy – the furniture so polished you could see your face in it. They didn't go in for modern furniture. Theirs had been handed down from parents and grandparents. They even had a grand piano in the lounge which no-one ever touched as they were not a musical family. But Dr Gruber, a struggling eccentric scientist who was a beautiful pianist, had only an ancient upright piano and the pride of his possessions, a really old harp.

The Grubers were not very often invited into the Baker home although Robert Baker and Mark Gruber were great friends. Mary always found herself rather on edge when she was talking to Nora. Nora was so sophisticated that Mary found her bristles coming up like a porcupine, as if she had to defend her way of life and the fact that she had no interest in anything except her home and children. She was the opposite of Nora who always looked so smart, even when doing her housework. Mary was aware of the contrast between her own dowdy, mousey appearance and Nora's smart, attractive clothes and her long black hair swept back into a pony tail. Even in these days of hardship Nora still managed to look immaculate.

'Hallo Nora,' called Mary, always eager for a chat.

'How are you managing?' replied Nora. 'Do you have any food?'

Mary looked surprised. It wasn't like Nora to ask how they were. 'I think I can just scrape up enough to make a meal for us today. How about you?'

'Don said this morning I should start packing a few things.'

'Whatever for?' said Mary, startled. 'Are you leaving him?'

'Oh no,' cried Nora. 'Don says there's no point in staying here, we shall only starve to death.'

Mary looked aghast at her – was the poor woman going out of her mind?

'Oh, I'm sure things will improve soon,' she said in a placating tone and she started to clean her windows as if life was the same as it always had been and she could wipe away such thoughts while cleaning the grime off the windows and seeing them come up clean and shining. After all, she

6

thought, hadn't there been hard times in the past when her husband was a struggling scientist and hadn't they always come through? She wrung out the cloth and began to polish the windows with even more fervour.

Nora went into the garage and looked around for the old garden wheelbarrow. There it was in the corner amongst a lot of garden tools. She got hold of the handle and recoiled at the touch of cobwebs festooned around the barrow. Although fastidious, Nora was an intelligent woman and realised that her husband was probably right and that things would never be the same as they used to be. Tears rolled down her cheeks at the thought of having to leave her beautiful home. She pulled the barrow out of the garage, scraping the old Jag. It passed fleetingly through her mind what wonderful times they'd had in that car.

Trips down to the sea when Robbie was little. She could see him so excited. 'Can I have a bucket and spade, Mummy?' he would cry.

'Yes of course,' she would reply, not realising what fun those days really were, watching Don getting down on his hands and knees helping to make sand castles and Robbie shrieking with delight as the waves trickled into the moat round the castle and then looking so crestfallen when a big wave would come and drown all their hard work.

'Well, this isn't getting on with the work. It's no good looking back. Don is right, we must move on; it's life or death.' With a final jerk she got the barrow out onto the path. Then she stood and ran her fingers through her hair in a perplexed manner. 'What the Hell have I got the wheelbarrow out for?' Suddenly she remembered. 'Of course, Don said we could only take as much stuff as we could get into a wheelbarrow.' All the same, they couldn't set off for a distant land with a wheelbarrow. She felt like laughing but then saw Mary looking over the fence at her with a vexed expression.

'Why don't you come with us?' cried Nora.

'No,' said Mary, tight lipped, 'this is my home and this is where I'm going to stay with my husband and my children.'

'Perhaps you might change your mind when you hear what Don has to say.'

'I won't. Things are bound to get better, they always do.'

7

Mary picked up her pail and cloth. The thought of leaving her home was unthinkable and she shut her mind to such nonsense.

'We'll see you tonight anyway,' shouted Nora.

'Perhaps,' replied Mary as she went in and shut the door.

Nora sighed and also went in to sort out a few things to take with them.

2

You could hear a pin drop in Dr Gruber's astronomical laboratory. He was sitting in front of a computer screen with headphones on. Above it all along the wall was a conglomeration of lights and push buttons. On another wall was a queer array of tiny loudspeakers attached to bits of wire resembling guitar strings, and above each speaker was a picture of a different instrument. It was Dr Gruber's pet experiment. The answer to space travel he knew must be in sound waves. He also knew, as did all scientifically-minded people, that the end of the planet was imminent as far as people were concerned.

They were waiting for the inevitable flood from the North Pole, a deluge which would be unprecedented in the planet's history. It would, of course, wipe out all civilisation, making, as it were, a clean sweep and maybe in a few thousand years' time other beings would evolve. Only a few stalwarts like Gruber, Benson and Campbell felt there was always a way out if one could find it.

Dr George Gruber was a small man, old for his forty years, with a prematurely lined face, greying hair already receding, but his eyes were as bright as a blackbird's. He was dressed in baggy trousers and jacket with an old roll neck sweater, all in dreary grey and black. They looked even more incongruous with the bright blue plastic shoes which belonged to his son Mark, who just left his shoes lying about in the hall and he had absent mindedly put his feet into them by mistake.

Dr Gruber didn't care what he looked like – most of the time he appeared to live in another world, which incidentally was what he was hoping to do. 'Another planet,'

9

he thought, 'similar to our own which we could colonise,' and his mind dwelt for a moment on those brave pioneering people who went out to America in the sixteenth century with no idea of what they were going to find. He did not, however, think that perhaps his new planet might be already inhabited, which, if it was like Earth, would seem quite possible. 'The answer must be in sound waves.'

All of a sudden he came out of his reverie. His face lit up as he became aware of a strange sound coming through the headphones. At the same time the computer bleeped and some of the strings emitted an eerie twanging noise. The computer was Dr Gruber's own invention, monitoring not only the solar system but all the stars in the galaxy up to a fifty thousand light year radius. He had, of course, heard many sound waves from various phenomena in the galaxy but this was the first time a light had come up on the screen. He trembled with excitement. It must, he thought, be a sound wave compatible with that of earth.

He watched the screen as a formation of stars began to appear. Suddenly the door was thrust open and Jim Benson strode in. He was a man of medium height with brown curly hair and a short retroussé nose. He was dressed in normal clothes for the year 1994, an all-in-one suit in plastic, dark blue material. He was the opposite of Gruber, looking so normal he would never have attracted a moment's attention from anyone.

'Gruber, what the hell's happened?' He thought perhaps Gruber had gone mad over this idea of his.

Gruber, wild-eyed, flung off the headphones and danced up and down shouting. 'I've got it, I've got it.'

'For Christ's sake man, calm down and stop behaving like a dancing dervish,' drawled Benson, trying not to appear perturbed.

'You don't understand, Benson. This is it. . . what we've been waiting for all these years. . . the breakthrough.'

Benson looked at the screen and saw the light pulsating near one of the stars. 'It's coming from the Constellation of Lyra, good God.' His attitude changed immediately as he realised that Gruber was not insane. This was indeed a moment of triumph. Here was hope.

'Put the headphones on and listen,' said Gruber and

handed them over.

Benson took the headphones and just as he did so the door opened and Alan Campbell appeared. 'Benson, they're waiting for you to lecture on electro. . .' He tailed off as he saw the light on the screen. He watched Benson's face change as a look of wonder suffused his face.

'It's fantastic,' he said with a note of awe. 'Here,' he beckoned to Campbell to listen. Campbell took the headphones from him. All thoughts of the students waiting impatiently for their lecture left their minds.

Campbell was a short man with dark, straight hair, worn like a medieval page boy. Also in his forties, he had been educated in Edinburgh but had left his wife and met a ravishing young science teacher. Hence, he found himself a post at the college and a bungalow nearby so they could live and work together. He was a jealous man and so made sure his Vikki had very little time to herself. There were several attractive young male students who fancied her. So when Benson said firmly, 'Someone will have to go over and take that lecture or we'll have them rampaging over here,' Campbell put down the headphones.

'You're right, I'll see if Vikki is free,' he said and rushed out.

The laboratory was part of the Scientific Experimental Complex and the local authority had only agreed to it to keep Dr Gruber quiet. They thought it was one way of keeping that madman out of the way. Gruber took up the headphones and listened. 'It's music all right, but all jangled up.'

Benson sat down in a chair next to him watching the screen intently. 'Perhaps it's each planet round that star giving out a different sound and the star in the middle is the synthesiser.'

Gruber nodded his head in agreement. Campbell rushed back in. 'It's O.K. Vikki has taken the class,' he said, breathing heavily.

'So now,' said Benson, 'not only do we know which planet would be habitable but we are well on the way to finding the means to get there.'

'Yes,' said Gruber excitedly. 'After all, it boils down to something relatively simple. All we have to do is adapt some

11

form of space craft with the identical sound to what we've just heard.'

Campbell interrupted. 'You mean connect the sounds by an electromagnetic wave which at the identical moment of contact will give it the thrust to leave the ground?'

'And that will give us almost instantaneous travel,' added Benson.

'Exactly,' said Gruber, deep in thought. 'I'd better get on to Professor Ascher. I'll use the office next door. Keep an eye on the screen and monitor the wavelengths,' he said as he went out.

'So, the others were on the wrong tack all the time trying to get over the speed of light,' said Benson.

'Yes,' replied Campbell. 'What we have to do now is get a spacecraft built with a propulsion that sounds the same as the sound waves coming from that planet.'

Benson was just about to say something when Gruber returned looking rather worried. 'I couldn't get hold of Ascher.'

'Perhaps he's given up,' said Benson. 'I can just imagine him rowing across the Atlantic with a boat full of instruments.'

'Or maybe he's struck the right chord on his harp and is flying across,' chuckled Campbell.

'Come, come,' said Gruber testily. 'This is no time for jokes. Time is of the essence.'

'Would you like me to go over to the College of Music and see if he's there?' said Benson placatingly.

'I'd better go and have a word with the electronics engineer, Matthews,' said Campbell.

'Good idea, yes, yes, go quickly,' Gruber replied to both of them. He wanted to concentrate on the weird sounds which seemed to be getting stronger and were filling the air with resonance, as if the speakers were too small to hold such musical vibration.

3

Benson and Campbell went out together and walked across the campus to the front gate where a few students were hanging about as if sensing that something was up. Quite a few of them were doing psychic research and were aware of such things. Benson and Campbell tried to speak nonchalantly. They knew it was no good getting everyone excited and then have the whole thing fizzle out. In any event, thinking of it in the cold light of day, it all seemed just too incongruous to be true.

'What do you think of it?' Benson asked Campbell, knowing that they were both thinking the same thoughts.

'Must say I'm too stunned to think anything,' replied Campbell.

'Theoretically it would seem possible.'

'But realistically?'

Benson shrugged his shoulders. 'Nothing ventured, nothing gained, I suppose.'

As they reached the gates one lanky youth leapt forward and opened the gate for them. 'Anything new cropped up, sir?'

'Nothing so far, my boy,' replied Benson.

'Some of us thought we heard something buzzing around in the air.'

'Most likely a wasp,' replied Campbell flippantly.

'Don't waste your time talking to them,' rasped a young girl. 'If they were going to another galaxy they wouldn't tell us.'

'Yeah, that's right,' was the general murmur.

Benson and Campbell almost ran through the gates which closed behind them with a loud clang. 'Phew, that was getting a bit close,' whispered Campbell.

'Shall I see you tonight at Gruber's?' Benson asked in a loud tone as if to dispel any thoughts that something unusual was up.

'I might look in later.'

They both thought it extremely unlikely that Gruber would be able to tear himself away from the laboratory. They parted company and Campbell made his way towards the large satellite dish in the field at the back of the college.

The Scientific Experimental College had only been founded for one year. It was an attempt to encourage all scientifically minded young people to conduct their own experiments in order to find some way of rescuing the human race from annihilation. The Government thought it a vain hope but at least the college kept a few people occupied and perhaps some genius might come up with something brilliant. Dr Gruber was the last person they would have considered to be in that league, which in a way gave him more scope as no-one took any real notice of what he was doing. All the professors and students knew the inevitability of extinction unless someone could find a practical way of evacuating the people to another planet, albeit, if this remote possibility did occur, only a select few would be chosen for such a dangerous hit or miss emigration. So far, of course, the problem had been in overcoming the speed of light.

It was considered most likely that those students studying psychic phenomena would have more chance of coming up with a solution to the problem of space travel than those studying the old-fashioned techniques of rocket propulsion, especially as there was no fuel left.

It had been said that one student, whose father had been strongly in favour of Jungian theories, put forward some far-fetched idea of concocting a giant astrological wheel with spokes which would point to all the different zodiacal constellations, and then by lying along the spoke appertaining to each person's individual sign, with sufficient deep meditation, they would be drawn to the constellation they were born under. An Aries person would automatically be drawn to the constellation of Aries, and so on. The fact that these constellations were thousands of light

14

years away did not deter those believers. With such a fraught situation, people were clutching at any straw.

Benson was thinking of this as he cycled along the dusty country road towards Greenham. He had been lucky enough to find an old bicycle propped against a tree when he came out of the college grounds which a student had forgotten to lock up. 'What rubbish,' he thought as he pedalled along. 'Maybe one could be reincarnated to a planet in one's sign of the Zodiac but not in this life. All the same, is that idea any more preposterous than Gruber's?'

There was an eerie feeling of foreboding as he cycled along the winding road. It was uncannily quiet. No birds were singing, no chickens squawking, and all the other country noises that used to fill the air. Then all of a sudden a large rat raced across the road just in front of him and then another and another. He almost came off the bike trying to miss them. Sweating with fear he managed to put a spurt on and pedalled furiously up the road. He looked round and breathed a sigh of relief when he saw they had not followed him. He felt sick but dared not get off and rest at the side of the road – supposing there were more rats?

'I must think of something more pleasant – I wonder if Professor Ascher has given up to find some desert oasis. If he has left England it will be a hopeless task to try and find him.' Benson knew that Ascher was very interested in Gruber's outrageous ideas and would come at the drop of a hat.

Benson, unlike Gruber and Campbell, lived on his own, his wife having gone off some years earlier with a meteorologist from North Africa. No doubt she saw it as a better chance of life, he thought. But surely too many people were rushing off to North Africa, having heard of the lush, green vegetation which was springing up. He imagined swarms of people converging on the oasis. 'No, not for me. I'll take my chances here with Gruber and Campbell.' He breathed heavily, trying not to drink in too much of the murky air. At last he was in sight of the college. There was hardly a soul about; an old woman crossing the road, a face peering behind a curtain, two cats fighting over a mouse.

He propped the bicycle up against the wall outside the college and hoped for the best that it would still be there

15

when he came out. He ran up the steps and pushed open the old front door which creaked and groaned. Benson thought of the times he had come here when music seemed to pour out of the very brickwork but now all he could hear was a ghostly echo. He went up the stairs to Professor Ascher's old room and gingerly knocked at the door.

'Come in,' croaked the Professor.

Benson entered the room and saw the old man hunched up in a large swivel chair. His hair was white and straggly but his face seemed remarkably unlined, having the delicate quality of someone not of this world. He had been doodling on a blank sheet of paper. All over the desk in front of him were scattered sheets of paper covered in crotchets and quavers. There was a piano in one corner of the room and various instruments were lying around.

There was a stultifying air of decay which made Benson want to go and open the old sash windows but the old man shivered and pointed to a chair. He leaned forward and peered over the top of his horn-rimmed spectacles. 'Sit down my boy and tell me your news.'

Benson felt like a messenger from times of yore bringing news of a siege but he knew he had to humour the old man. He sat down in a chair thick with dust. 'It's exciting news, Professor, and we want your help.'

The Professor perked up even more. Nobody had asked for his help for a very long time. He swivelled round in his chair, putting the fingertips of his bony hands together.

'Exciting, is it?' his eyes lost their glazed look.

'Yes, Gruber has had a breakthrough with his sound experiment. Can you come now to the laboratory?'

'Marvellous,' said the Professor rubbing his hands gleefully. 'Mind you, I'm not really up-to-date with what's going on nowadays.'

'I don't think that will matter,' replied Benson. 'We need some musical tones deciphered.'

'Well, that does sound right up my street.'

'I hoped you would say that.'

'Let's go, I've sat here long enough twiddling my thumbs,' and he jumped out of his chair. 'Come, you can tell me about it on the way,' he said as he led the way out of the room and almost flew down the stairs, his enthusiasm

16

lending wings to his feet. Benson hurried after him.

4

Mary Gruber was a very round, comfortable looking woman in her early forties with fair hair cut short and a round face to match her generous proportions. She was not of an intellectual turn of mind and did not even begin to comprehend what her husband was doing. She only knew that life was getting increasingly difficult. There were no shops any more and it came through on the home computer each morning what food was available, and then it meant going to the Old Town Hall to queue. It was getting now that people were so desperate for food they had no manners at all. Everybody pushed and shoved to get the best portions and sometimes there wasn't enough to go round. That morning she had collected barely enough to make a meal for herself and her husband and their two children, Mark aged fourteen and Katie, ten. She tried not to complain as everyone was in the same boat. Even those people who were very rich now found that with all their money there was no extra or better food to be had.

'In fact,' she thought to herself, 'perhaps it's easier for the poor folks to survive, not having been used to the rich, succulent meals of the past.' Money seemed to be completely useless. 'Well, no good thinking about it, I must get on with making some sort of meal for the children. God knows when that husband of mine will come in – I can't think what he gets up to all day messing about in that laboratory of his. Still, it gives him something to do, I suppose.'

She looked up from wiping the kitchen table in readiness for the meagre repast as Katie came in, a rather small child with long blonde hair like her mother's had once been.

18

'I'm hungry, Mum,' she said and sat down at the table. 'Where's Mark?'

'I don't know,' replied Katie. 'He stayed behind talking to some guys at the survival class. They say the end of the world is coming very soon,' she said nonchalantly, putting her elbows on the table and cupping her little face in her hands, waiting to see her mother's reaction to this remark.

'People have been saying that for hundreds of years,' she said, although she could not help a shudder running down her spine. This, on top of what Nora said this morning. Her hand trembled slightly as she got four plates down from the shelf of the old fashioned dresser. It had belonged to her husband's mother and he never would agree to their getting rid of it and having something more modern.

'There's no substitute for wood,' he would say. Somehow she had always felt there was something not quite right about that remark.

'You shouldn't listen to such silly talk, Katie,' she said, but even as the words came out of her mouth the plates rattled on the table. She rummaged in the plastic bag amongst the pitiful selection of vegetables and brought out four pathetic-looking potatoes, going green with shoots coming out of them, and four carrots, one onion and four eggs. Mark opened the door. He was short, taking after his father, with dark, curly hair. He flung himself down on a chair at the table.

'What's to eat, Mum?' he cried.

He threw his school bag on the floor, spilling books and pens. He pushed his chair back to pick them up and promptly trod on his best pen. 'Clumsy idiot,' taunted Katie.

'We're lucky today, I managed to get four eggs so we can have a vegetable omelette,' said Mrs Gruber.

She took the vegetables and put them in a bowl in the sink, took a saucepan out of the cupboard under the draining board and picked up a small knife to peel them.

'So, big brain,' said Katie to Mark, 'when is the world coming to an end?'

'Wouldn't you like to know,' he mocked.

'Now you two, don't start,' said Mrs Gruber wearily as she cut up the vegetables into small pieces.

'I'll throw this egg on the floor if you don't tell me,' shouted Katie.

'No,' shrieked Mrs Gruber. 'That's all we have to eat today,' and she lunged forward to grab the egg from Katie's hand. Katie let go of the egg and they all looked in horror as the egg fell and splattered onto the floor.

'You stupid fool,' shouted Mark, leaping up and hitting Katie on the head. Just as Mrs Gruber managed to get hold of the other eggs before they went the same way there was a light knock at the door.

'I'll go,' said Katie, glad of the diversion so that she could get away from her brother. She ran out of the kitchen to answer the front door. Nora's cat had jumped in through the kitchen window and was busy licking up the egg from the floor. There was never any food left over to give to pets. 'In fact,' thought Mary, 'the shortage of cats makes me wonder.' Before she could wonder any further, Katie ran back into the kitchen.

'There's a horrid looking man at the door,' she said. 'He looks like a tramp.'

'Everybody looks like a tramp now,' retorted Mark scathingly.

Mary went to the door and saw a man with clothes ragged and dirty hanging from his thin frame like a scarecrow. 'I can't go on. . . the dinosaurs. . .' He slumped in a heap on the doorstep. The others came into the hall and looked at this sorry sight.

'Look,' shouted Mark, 'a wallet has fallen out of his pocket.'

'What funny clothes he's got on,' said Katie, inspecting the torn jacket.

Mark picked up the wallet but Mary snatched it from him. 'Give it to me,' she said.

Mary opened the wallet and found it contained a photograph of a nice looking woman and a printed card which read 'P. Marsden – Special Pass. ANC Government Official. No.9152' She put the wallet into her own pocket and looked round at them.

'What's it say, Mum?' chorused Katie and Mark in unison.

'Nothing much,' said Mary. 'I'll give it to your father

20

when he comes in.'

Together Mark and Mary managed to drag the man inside the house and pulled him onto a low seat by the window. 'Get some water,' said Mary to Katie. All thoughts of food were now forgotten in the excitement and Katie obediently went to fetch the glass of water.

The man spluttered as they tried to get the water into his mouth through the ragged foliage of beard and moustache. 'He's coming round,' said Mark.

The man opened his eyes and looked around. Just then there was another knock at the door – this time it was Nora, Don and Robert. Mark let them in.

'What's going on?' said Robert, looking with great interest at the spectacle.

'Some tramp just fell on the doorstep,' said Mark.

'He doesn't half stink,' said Robert succinctly.

Mary looked up. 'Hallo Nora, this poor man has collapsed.'

'He sure looks in a bad way,' said Don.

Nora was fascinated and repulsed at the same time.

'I must phone George and get him to come home,' said Mary as she went out into the hall.

'Where have you come from?' said Don to the man.

'What's your name?' chipped in Katie.

'Philip. Philip Marsden,' he said.

Everyone gathered round him to listen to his story. He opened his mouth as if to speak then looked at the gathering round him – the young children waiting with bated breath, Don and Nora Baker looking perplexed and not knowing what to do or say. Nora sat down nervously.

'Where am I?' said Marsden cautiously.

'In Dr Gruber's house,' said Don.

'Good. That's just what I need, a doctor,' he breathed.

'Oh no, he's not a doctor, he's a scientist,' said Don.

At that, Marsden's ears pricked up and his eyes steeled. Mary came back into the room. 'George will be here in a minute,' she said soothingly.

Dr Gruber, Benson and the Professor arrived together and joined the throng, trying to listen to everyone talking at once about what had happened. 'What's all this?' asked Gruber impatiently, looking at Marsden. The last thing he wanted now was some lame duck getting in the way when he was bursting to get on with his discovery.

Professor Ascher sat down at the harp and strummed away, completely disinterested in what was going on. He too couldn't wait to work something out of Gruber's experiment. Mary handed the wallet to her husband.

'Daddy,' Katie grabbed his arm, 'he's seen a dinosaur.'

Gruber hardly heard. 'Where have you come from?' he said abruptly to Marsden.

Don broke in rapidly, bored with this scene. 'We came to see if you were interested in coming with us tomorrow. We're off, there's no point in staying here. There may be hope somewhere else.'

'There's no hope anywhere else,' said Gruber roughly — then, less harshly, 'There may be hope but it certainly won't be on this planet.'

Everyone gaped. Don looked fed up. Here was Gruber going off again on his crazy ideas. 'Well, I'm not going to sit here waiting for the end. I'm going tomorrow.' He looked at Nora. Robert and Mark were listening in to the home computer and did not hear him.

'I don't know,' faltered Nora. 'Perhaps Dr Gruber is right, maybe we should wait a bit.' Nora had always admired George Gruber and thought Mary was far too stupid to be married to such a brilliant man. Her loyalties wavered.

Robert then piped in, hearing his mother's last remark. 'I want to stay here. I don't want to leave my friends.'

For Nora that was enough. 'Don't let's go tomorrow, Don,' she pleaded.

Don was adamant. 'It's tomorrow or not at all,' he said.

Gruber looked round angrily and said to Benson and Professor Ascher, 'Come, let's get back to the laboratory. I left Campbell and Matthews in charge.'

'We'd better take him with us,' said Benson looking at Marsden, who seemed to have revived after Mary had found a packet of dried soup which she had been saving and which she had managed to get down him. Benson and Gruber helped Marsden up and walked him to the door. Professor Ascher followed. Katie and Mark both tried to grab the cup of soup to see if there was any left. Don and

Nora left with Robert. Mary could still hear them arguing after the door had slammed shut. All of a sudden she felt very lonely.

5

What had not been made generally known to the public was the fact that when the earth tilted, the water from the English Channel had completely swamped the Isle of Wight. Although now drained away into the Atlantic Ocean it had left pockets of water, creating small and large lakes. Also, the cliffs had given way and after many landslides, large caves had appeared and what was left of the Channel Tunnel, which had never been finished, became an underground cave which was now a breeding ground for all types of fish.

Giant turtles had been seen. One poor child had been considered a lying little scaremonger through reporting such a tale. Most of the people in that area had been drowned together with all the animals. Only rats ran amok and, of course, now that the ground had dried up it was crawling with insects as there were no predators.

Except in one cave where something very strange had happened. Where thousands of tons of earth had suddenly disintegrated there came to light a nest of huge eggs, as if preserved in ice. In a short time the rays of the sun had hatched out these eggs and out slithered several healthy baby dinosaurs. It was not long before these babies were crawling around inspecting their surroundings just as if they had not been sealed up for millions of years, incarcerated in the depths of the earth.

There seemed to be plenty of green stuff left where the sea had covered the earth and the dinosaurs lived and thrived. They started roaming further and further north. Anyone looking down from the air would have thought they were back in the beginning of time. The dinosaurs' great legs stomped and their tails swished as if they were really enjoying this rebirth. Philip Marsden had seen these creatures.

On the way from Dr Gruber's house to the laboratory, Philip began to remember what had happened. He had been working in a nuclear plant near the small village of Gorsley in Wiltshire. He lived in a flat in the special block provided for the employees of the plant. He was lying in bed reading when he heard the bleep bleep of his computer. He got up and went over to watch the message coming up on the screen. It was nearly midnight. He thought he must be dreaming as he read the words, 'State of Emergency – all personnel with the following numbers make their own way to . . .' and then a line of hieroglyphics which Philip quickly wrote down. He recognised these as France, District Phase I. 'No travel facilities available'. A list of numbers was then given and Philip saw his own number come up. 'Good God, 9152, that's me,' he cried aloud. He looked at the screen but it had already gone blank. The message would not be put out again in case spies were able to decipher the code.

Most of the personnel at the plant had been told secretly that in case of emergency and total abandonment of the planet, a large airbus fully stocked with fuel and supplies would take off from a special airport in France to fly to the shuttle lift-off in America where, if you were lucky, you would get a place on a shuttle and be whisked off to the Shangri-la space station, as it was nicknamed.

Philip imagined that when it came to the last shuttle to leave the ground it would probably become a nightmare with all and sundry fighting to get on – no doubt there would be one or two without a pass who would hold up the pilot at gun point. Perhaps many of them would be the poor devils who had worked to save others and yet would not be able to get away themselves.

Philip realised that he had to think of something quickly if he was going to find a means of getting to France. He heard men shouting and running about, no doubt trying to think of some means of transport for themselves and their families as it would be a question of first come, first served. 'Lucky I'm not married,' he thought. 'He travels fastest who travels alone.'

25

Suddenly he thought of his old school friend Ben Hutton whom he had not seen for years. 'He used to live near here and his father had his own private plane.' Philip's heart quickened as the idea in his mind evolved. 'I wonder if he's still got it? . . . but does Ben still live there? . . . and then, would there be any fuel? . . . I'd better stop wondering and start walking. It's worth a try.'

Philip feverishly put on his anti-nuclear suit and boots, put a few necessary articles into a small rucksack and left the flat. He tried not to get stopped by people calling out to him. Having always been regimented and told exactly what to do, the majority were at a loss as to how to make their own way. They were looking for a leader. 'And it's not going to be me,' thought Philip selfishly. As he made his way along the corridor to the main stairs, doors opened and he could not dodge the questions . . .

'Hi, Philip, got any ideas?'

'Can we get together? . . .'

'How the Hell are we going to get to France?'

And the tap on the shoulder, the grab of his wrist as they shouted, 'Where are you off to? . . .'

'Sorry old boy,' muttered Philip as he dragged himself away from their clutching hands and their searching eyes. He tore down the stairs and out of the front door, plunging blindly into the darkness. He was not usually so hard and oblivious of other people's feelings but, as is so often the case when it comes to life or death, the basic instincts of survival over-rode the normal sympathies. 'It's every man for himself now,' he told himself, making excuses for his bad behaviour. He strode along the narrow country road towards his friend's house . . .

After nearly three hours' walking through the dark country lanes with only the faint light of the moon which appeared intermittently through the clouds and mist to light his way, he arrived at Ben's house. The lovely old house stood quite a way back from the road. It looked eerie in the pale moonlight. Philip peered through the wrought iron gate. A high wall encompassed the front and sides of the house. The once immaculate lawns leading up to the front of the house were now knee high and weeds trailed out of the cracks in the wall. What if Ben was no longer there? He pushed open the creaking gate, walked up to the front door and knocked loudly. A light appeared upstairs, the window opened and an anxious voice called out, 'Who's there?'

'It's Philip, Philip Marsden,' replied Philip hopefully.

Ben was delighted to hear the voice of his old friend. 'Come in old chap. Wait a jiff.'

Ben threw on an old dressing gown and leapt down the stairs. His sense of adventure which had lain dormant for so long swelled up. He knew Philip was a live wire and for him to come knocking at the door in the early hours of the morning meant something traumatic was afoot. 'What brings you here at this ungodly hour?' he asked as he opened the door.

'God, he's aged,' thought Philip as he looked at Ben's lined face and the dark hair going thin on top. His lean frame was not that of the once well-built athletic type he had been. But still, he seemed cheerful enough. Philip followed Ben into the lounge and sank back into an armchair facing the antique marble fireplace. 'It's good to sit down.'

'I'll see if I can rake up some tea or coffee.' Ben could see that Philip was tired out.

'Sounds great.'

Ben went into the kitchen and put the kettle on. Philip stretched his legs and looked round the room with its old maroon velvet curtains and old-fashioned furniture – the sideboard with the leaded windows and the cupboard underneath where Ben's father used to keep his whisky and soda. He remembered the good times he'd had with Ben and his father – playing snooker in the next room and darts, going fishing and the thrill of a ride in his private plane. Ben's father had been a wealthy industrialist and had his own plane, flying being his favourite hobby. This thought promptly brought him back to the reason why he was now sitting in this chair in Ben's house.

Ben came in carrying two mugs of black coffee. 'All I could find. Good thing Dad used to be a hoarder. . .'

Philip cut in. 'Used to be . . ?'

'Poor old Dad had a heart attack last year – he was chopping down a tree for firewood – I think it was too much for him. I didn't realise how frail he was getting.' Ben choked on the words; he had been so close to his Dad.

'I'm sorry,' said Philip, crestfallen. Did this mean that his plan was now obsolete?

'I was just remembering what good times we used to have – have you still got the snooker table?'

'I should say so – it's a bit dog-eared but we'll have a game later. . .'

'I'd better tell you why I'm here,' said Philip hurriedly. Ben listened intently to Philip's news and then realised why he had come.

'Have you still got the old plane?' asked Philip in trepidation.

'As a matter of fact, we have.' Ben spoke as if his father was still about. 'And it's not that old. Dad had the latest Dove model. He used it not long ago.'

Philip's hopes rose again. 'Do you think you could fly it?'

'Well, I never did pass the test, couldn't be bothered. I suppose I'm not that keen on flying myself so I never got my licence.'

'Who gives a shit about a licence now – it's every man for himself,' said Philip savagely.

'Of course, old chap.' Ben was a little taken aback at Philip's tone. Philip saw the look on Ben's face and realised he would have to be a little more tactful and not so aggressive in his speech.

'What I mean is, there are no planes flying anywhere so the sky is clear, so to speak.'

'Hadn't thought of that.'

'So, what do you think? Want to have a bash?'

'Sure.' Ben was eager to get started, reassured that he would not be breaking any laws. 'I'll go and get some suitable gear on.' He looked at Philip as if seeing him for the first time. 'What on earth is that you're wearing?'

'Oh, it's just a special bad weather suit,' said Philip glibly, but inwardly felt rather ashamed at the way he was using his old friend.

Ben accepted his explanation without question and went upstairs to get dressed. Philip breathed a sigh of relief. 'I suppose he's not fully aware of the implications of what I've just told him, living in this backwater.' Why, there wasn't even a television in the room. 'No wonder he's not up to date.'

He looked at his watch. 'Come on Ben, perhaps we can still make it but I doubt if I'll be able to get you onto the shuttle without a pass.' He put that thought to the back of his mind. After a few moments Ben returned, all zipped up in his old flying suit.

'Ready old chap?'

'Right,' said Philip as he jumped out of the chair.

The enormity of what they were proposing to do gave them both zest and energy. Ben shut the front door after him with a bang as if he knew he would never see his home again. They started walking, both thinking their own thoughts. It was a gloomy start to the day, a strange mist hung around the half dead trees. The hedges were threadbare and the grass was a yellowish colour. It used to be green and lush where the cows and sheep had grazed, chewing happily and giving rich milk, wool and meat.

Ben could remember going into the kitchen of the farmhouse where he had lived with his father. His mother had died when he was two years old and he had been brought up by his father and an elderly nanny who spoiled him; plus, of course, all the other staff needed to run such a big estate. He could almost smell the lovely steak and kidney pies and roast dinners that cook used to put on the table.

As they made their way across the fields, Ben looked back at the house and thought of the times when he was a boy and he had looked out of his bedroom window to see his father taking off or landing the piane on their own private runway. Not looking where he was going he trod on a rabbit rotting on the ground. 'Could have made myself a rabbit stew,' he thought. It was amazing that no-one had found it. Rabbit would be a luxury now. He tried not to think of food. If he could manage to get the plane off the ground he presumed that he would be able to go with Philip on this special mission. Although Philip thought he was completely clueless about what was going on, he did know through a friend who worked in a Government Office that THEY had been getting a space station ready for years so that they could make a quick get-away in case of nuclear attack or natural disaster. And, as it so happened, it was the latter which struck. He knew it was a mini-earth with soil, trees, animals and all the essentials to grow food. Plus it would be crammed with tinned and frozen food – not the one dinner a day capsule being dished out to people to stop starvation.

Philip was also thinking along these lines — he could imagine succulent roast lamb with potatoes and fresh peas and maybe even mint sauce. If they could just get to La Baune in time for the airbus, that awful journey in the shuttle would seem like a magic carpet whisking them off to the Garden of Eden.

Both men came down to earth as they approached the hangar. Ben unbolted and pulled open the door which creaked and groaned as they entered. 'It must be over a year since Dad took her up and I doubt if we've got enough juice to fly her anyway.' Ben patted the Dove affectionately.

'Here, what's this?' cried Philip exultantly. 'There's enough here to get us to La Baune.' He uncovered several large canisters stacked in a corner of the hangar. 'Do you think it's still O.K?' Philip shook one of the canisters.

Ben was surveying the plane. He looked round, suddenly remembering. 'Oh yes, it'll be all right. Dad knew some scientist who came up with a substance which would keep petrol and oil for two or three years. Poor old Dad never knew if it worked or not. Neither, I suppose,' he ruminated, 'did the chap who invented it.'

'Well, now's the time to find out. Here, give me a hand,' and Philip started rolling one of the canisters towards the plane.

'Even if the fuel is O.K. it will still be a miracle if I can get her off the ground.'

'Don't be so pessimistic.' Nothing must stop them now.

'I've never flown the plane without Dad,' Ben continued. He was beginning to have a few qualms about his prowess as a pilot. Philip did not want to know about his fears.

'There's no time to hang about, come on, let's fill her up.'

'Right,' agreed Ben. He accepted that he should have a go at the seemingly impossible. After all, what was there to lose?

They managed to get every drop of fuel into the plane.

30

Then they got in and strapped themselves in. Ben checked the controls and after much jumping and juddering, the plane taxied across the field and down the runway. They were both amazed when they found themselves in the air. Philip looked at his watch. It was now 9 a.m. There was still time. The deadline was noon.

They both remained silent, hardly daring to speak. 'Mustn't congratulte ourselves too soon,' thought Philip, on edge in case something else went wrong.

After they had been flying for about twenty minutes, cruising nicely, there was a sudden bang and the plane began to lose height rapidly. Ben struggled with the controls and tried to make a forced landing. 'Oh God, we're going to land in the chasm,' yelled Philip.

But as luck would have it, the plane zoomed down, running along the edge of the cliff top and striking a convenient tree which stopped them from going straight down the cliff. Ben had passed out. Philip was shaken but not hurt. 'Poor devil.' Philip gave Ben a shake but he did not flicker an eyelid. 'I suppose he's had a heart attack.'

Philip was eaten up with frustration at having got so near to an escape. He unstrapped himself and climbed out of the plane. He looked over the precipice and saw what had been the English Channel. The cliff face was muddy and further down he could see jagged pieces of rock sticking out. Many people had tried to climb down the cliff only to fall, cut and bleeding, at the bottom. A few had made it and were trying to wade their way through mud and slime. 'What chance have they got to get to the Continent?' he thought. 'Poor sods don't realise they're doomed.' Philip looked round, not knowing which direction to take. He walked along a path which appeared to lead into a wood.

He stopped and sat down for a while, beginning to feel tired and weak after all these traumatic events. He was also feeling guilty about leaving Ben and wondered if he should go back to make sure he had not revived. Suppose even now Ben was calling for him? 'No, he had a fatal stroke,' Philip reassured himself, and with renewed determination dragged himself onto his feet and followed the path into the wood. It was then that he got the fright of his life. He stood frozen to the spot as he watched a gigantic dinosaur

31

rampaging through the trees, emitting a hoarse cry which was indescribable, and behind it another smaller one came leaping after it.

Philip could not believe his eyes. 'Perhaps I did have a bump on the head after all, or maybe it is a fantasy dream, after all I've had no sleep all night.'

He looked around fearfully. There was no sign of any more dinosaurs.

He shrugged his shoulders. 'Oh, what the Hell, why worry about dinosaurs anyway, they only eat leaves,' he thought philosophically, whereupon he slung his bag over his shoulder and plodded on. Although he was aware that most dinosaurs were vegetarian, he also knew that he could be trodden underfoot just the same as he would tread on an ant without even seeing it. Anyway, if he was dreaming then at least he would wake up soon.

He plodded on through the forest, along muddy lanes, through villages which looked as if the black death had struck; those people who had not died of illness or starvation had died simply of hopelessness. All the hospitals had closed down. People had to cope as best they could with their illnesses. Operations were a thing of the past. 'Really, I suppose it's just like living in the first century, except they were luckier, they had good food and fresh, pure air to breathe. It must have been good to have been alive in those days. Better to live in a cave with good food than live in a beautiful house and starve,' he ruminated. But Philip persevered. 'Where there's life, there's hope,' he thought stoically. Eventually he arrived at the Gruber's house exhausted, hungry and dirty, to collapse on their doorstep.

6

Don and Nora were still arguing. Don was looking angrily out of the window. Nora was slumped on the settee feeling exhausted and confused. Now it came to the crunch she was not sure that Don was right. Could Mary's attitude be the right one after all? Was it best to ignore what was happening and pretend that everything was quite normal?

Robert was looking at the television. There were no entertainment programmes but every now and again a map of the world would come up with signs and symbols displayed underneath so that you could see which parts of the world were under water and which were still habitable.

'Mum, Dad, look at this,' yelled Robert. They both looked at the screen and their faces were full of fear.

'The flood from the Arctic is heading for Iceland and then it will be coming straight for England. We must go quickly while we have a chance,' said Don nervously.

'But where can we go?' whined Nora.

'Anywhere.'

'But the flood will catch up with us whichever way we go,' piped up Robert.

'It's worth trying. If we went south east we might be able to get to North Africa.'

Don felt more optimistic. Yes, that was it. North Africa.

'How are you going to cross the Channel?' enquired Nora.

'There isn't any Channel now, Mum. Look, it has disappeared.'

'You're right, Rob, there's no water between here and France.'

'That's just what I'm trying to tell you. We can walk,' said

Don, even more exasperated.

'It must have happened when the earth moved on its axis,' said Robert.

'It's the first time they've shown that on the screen.'

'Oh, never mind what they're showing,' said Don impatiently. 'Come on. Let's get going. Did you find the sleeping bags in the garage?'

'Oh dear.' Nora suddenly realised what she had been looking for in the garage but she had been so taken up with reminiscing she had forgotten all about the sleeping bags and camping gear.

'I suppose I'll have to look for them. You two, get yourselves together. Take some warm clothes and extra shoes. What do you say?' Don pleaded.

He did not really want to go on such a trek alone. Nora thought for a minute. 'I still think we should wait and see what Dr Gruber has come up with,' she said quietly.

Don became angry again. 'That's just a pipe dream. We all know he's mad but no-one dares admit it.'

Robert hotly came to Dr Gruber's defence. 'He's not mad.'

'Well, perhaps that's a bit strong. Anyway, do you think if he has found some way of getting away from here he'll be able to take us with him?'

'D'you mean to another planet?' Robert's eyes glowed with excitement.

'Another planet? Well, that does seem a bit far-fetched,' agreed Nora.

'Huh, he's off his rocker. The only thing to do in a situation like this is to think of something practical.'

Robert's imagination had been fired. 'I want to go to another planet. I don't think much of this one anyway.'

'Don't be silly,' said Don roughly. 'It would only be rocks and stones and we'd starve anyway.'

'How do you know?' cried Robert and Nora in unison.

'Better the devil you know,' said Don quietly.

He mustn't lose his rag or they would never get anywhere.

'I suppose it's better than doing nothing.' Nora was torn between agreeing with either of them. She really did not want to part with Don. He was a bit pig-headed but, for all

34

that, a good man.

'I'm the only one who wants to do something. I shall walk half way round the world if necessary.' And with that, Don stormed out of the room shouting, 'I'm going to find the sleeping bags. Are you coming or not?'

Nora and Robert looked at each other. 'What do you think, Robert?' her voice faltered.

Nora was near to tears. She felt such a decision was just too much. How could she take such responsibility for herself and Robert? Don had always made the big decisions of life for them. Nora's life had been so placid, doting parents who now lived in Australia with her older sister. Nora had met Don when they emigrated so she stayed behind in a nice flat in London until they married and moved to the country. From then on she was involved with her work as a beautician in the neighbouring town of Kirby; happy enough for Don to decide whether or not they should stay in England or go to Australia. 'Now,' she thought, 'perhaps we should have gone after all, things might be better there.' There was no post or overseas communications so she realised she might never see her family again.

'Mum,' Robert interrupted her reverie.

'Yes. Have you made up your mind then?'

Robert, too, was at a loss. He was used to his parents telling him what to do. 'I don't know – I suppose we should go with Dad but it seems pretty hopeless to try and walk to Africa.'

'I must say I agree with that.'

'And then perhaps Dr Gruber *might* come up with something,' pleaded Robert.

Although the idea of another planet seemed ridiculous, Nora could not help feeling nervously excited. Why not wait a day or two and see what happened?

'I don't want to leave my friends,' cried Robert passionately. He had just thought how he would miss his friend Mark and maybe even Katie, although she was a perishing little nuisance at times.

'Nor do I,' agreed Nora. She knew what they were going to do. 'We'll stay with our friends.'

Before this desperate situation she would never have

thought of Mary as her friend.

'I'll go and see what your Dad's doing. Maybe we can persuade him to stay.'

7

When Dr Gruber, Benson, Marsden and Professor Ascher entered the laboratory they found Campbell with the electronics engineer, Matthews. Campbell was explaining the computer and sound system to him. Ray Matthews was a Jamaican who had only recently joined the college. It was common knowledge that he was having an affair with Campbell's girlfriend, the voluptuous redhead, Vikki. Vikki did not appear to slot into the category of a lecturer on physics. She seemed more sympathetic to the course on psychic studies. Matthews was well aware that if Campbell learnt about the affair he was a dead man, but he was a philosophical character who liked to take on dangerous assignments and merely thought there were worse ways to go. He hoped it wouldn't come to that, as he really liked Campbell.

Philip Marsden slumped into a chair out of the scientists' way. He dozed off and let the sounds and conversation drone on around him. The others grouped around the computer, watching the star cluster intently. The Professor put his ear first to one of the tiny speakers and then another, trying to decipher the various tones. He started dancing about in quite a maniacal manner.

'Give me a pen and paper quickly,' he cried. Benson took a small notebook and pencil from his jacket pocket.

'No, no, I need some large paper.'

'Here you are Professor.' Gruber handed him a large pile of scrap paper which he had been using for his own notes. The Professor feverishly started drawing crotchets and quavers. 'It seems to be in a major key,' he said, his eyes sparkling.

'How does that affect us?' asked Gruber.

'It means that this planet you've found should be a joyful place.'

'Super,' said Gruber. But then the smile went from his face. 'How can it be a major key if our planet is in a minor key?'

'That's a good point,' said Benson.

'Yes,' joined in Campbell. 'Can you explain how we are connecting? We were working on the theory that for space travel, a planet would have to emit an identical sound.'

Gruber rubbed his chin. 'Unless it could work on an opposite vibration.'

'Hey, Matthews,' called Benson, 'you're very quiet. What's ticking over in that brain of yours?'

'Well,' replied Matthews, 'I was just wondering if perhaps a positive planet will only communicate with a negative one. After all, nothing moves without friction.'

'Bravo,' said Campbell.

'Perhaps that's why we haven't been able to make contact before, we've been looking for an identical sound instead of an opposite one,' mused Gruber.

'But there would still have to be an underlying sound which is identical,' Benson argued.

'That's it,' Matthews' brain was working fast. 'Whereas the waves of this planet are under the line of the identical sound, the twin planet would have sound waves above the line.'

'Interconnecting on each wave,' added Benson.

'So the sound would make one continuous wave.'

'Fantastic,' said Campbell.

They all breathed a sigh of relief that this hurdle had been overcome.

Meanwhile, no-one had taken any notice of Marsden. Although he had been asleep most of the time during the conversation that was going on, he had managed to get the gist of what they were trying to do. He had been dreaming that a large dinosaur was chasing after him through the woods and just as a large foot was about to come crashing down on him he woke up. 'I'd better try and keep awake and listen to this,' he thought. 'All the same, it might be best if they think I'm asleep.' So he closed his eyes again.

The Professor was still listening intently to the sounds. Suddenly he spoke. 'The instrument to be used is the harp.'

Gruber was ecstatic. 'Is that because it's coming from the constellation of Lyra?'

'That means a harp doesn't it?' queried Benson.

'You're thinking of the lyre.'

'Maybe the ancients knew a lot more than we give them credit for,' added Campbell.

'I think these sounds will make a musical phrase,' muttered the Professor.

'Marvellous.'

'Super.'

'God's teeth.'

'One would have thought it would have to be an electronic instrument,' Matthews said in a sceptical tone.

'Only because that's what we've been led to believe,' replied Gruber.

'Perhaps we shall find ourselves in Heaven instead of on another planet,' said Campbell in a jocular tone.

'It probably will be Heaven after this earth.'

The Professor was quite oblivious to the remarks going back and forth around him and seemed to be in another world already. This had given him new life. Not only to be of use but to be translating the music emanating from another planet was beyond his wildest dreams. He was now the most important person in this experiment. If he could not decipher the musical code, who could? Gruber was a good musician but he played by ear.

Marsden now thought it was about time he chipped in. 'Don't you think you guys had better come down to earth for a bit. Suppose you do manage to reconstruct the exact sounds of another planet, what vehicle are you going to use? There's no spacecraft here.'

They all looked at him, apart from the Professor, as if he had said something totally unreasonable. Gruber was first to speak. 'The whole idea doesn't rest on having a spacecraft, anything would do if it was reasonably secure and totally enclosed.'

'But I suppose the problem does still remain as to exactly what we could use,' agreed Campbell. 'It won't drop out of the blue.'

They looked at each other uneasily. Benson was still deep in thought. The question of a suitable vehicle had never even been discussed – mainly, of course, because deep down no-one had ever really thought that the experiment would succeed. Now that it had, they were at a loss. It would be futile to have the means of escape without the vehicle to take them. Also, it had to be something big enough to take several people. Apart from themselves, some women and children would have to be included.

Matthews also could not come up with a brilliant solution on the spot. 'I suppose they thought they would somehow just be spirited away on a sound wave like an ascension into Heaven,' he thought.

'Why don't you all try and work out that problem and the Professor and I will concentrate on the music,' suggested Gruber.

'Hold on,' said Benson. 'We're all in this together you know.' He was not too pleased with Gruber's nonchalant attitude.

'Who's got any ideas then?' enquired Campbell.

'As a matter of fact, I have,' Benson replied. 'I've had a theory buzzing in my head for some time. I think shape has something to do with it.'

They looked at him in amazement. Marsden was listening now with interest. What a hornet's nest he had stirred up. 'How can a shape give out a tune?'

'Have we got to bring geometry into it?'

The questions came thick and fast until Campbell chipped in, 'If we give each sound a shape as we connect the note into the synthesiser, all we have to do is depress those shapes with a laser and they should integrate into one shape.'

'And,' Benson continued, 'I think we shall find that the one big shape will be. . .'

Here they all joined in together as one voice, 'The brain!'

'I do believe you're right,' Gruber acknowledged, wishing he had thought of it himself.

Marsden eased himself out of the chair. 'I think I'll go outside for a breath of air.' After his sudden outburst he now felt too tired to think about it. 'Let them get on with it,' he thought. 'I can't be bothered any more.'

'Here, Professor, why don't you sit down for a while and have a nap?'

The old man yawned, 'I am a little tired now after all this excitement. Maybe I'll just have forty winks before I continue.'

Marsden went outside and walked slowly down to the gate. 'I've had enough of thinking about their high flung ideas. It's all too ridiculous to take seriously anyway.' He opened the gate and looked across the road towards Berry Hill. He could not believe his eyes. 'That looks like a plane. Surely it's not Ben?' He rushed back to the lab.

'Hush, not so much noise,' said Gruber, annoyed at the interruption.

'I'm sorry, but I'm sure a small plane has landed on the hill.'

'Perhaps we'd better go and have a look,' Campbell moved towards the door.

They all followed Marsden down to the gate.

'It's the answer to our prayers,' breathed Benson.

'It's Ben Hutton,' whispered Marsden.

They all looked at him, having forgotten in the excitement that they knew nothing about this man. Who was he? Where had he come from?

Campbell was the first to speak. 'Spill it, man.'

'Firstly, we'll go back to the lab,' said Gruber. So they all trooped back. Marsden looked round the faces staring at him accusingly, waiting for an answer.

'What does it matter if I tell them?' he thought. He looked at his watch. Yes, the airbus would have gone long ago and the shuttle was probably well on its way. So he started to tell them the whole story. Clearly and concisely he told them of the Government plan to take as many clever and useful people as possible up to the Mini Earth with a view to staying there long enough for things to simmer down and stabilise on planet Earth and eventually they would be able to come back and start again where they had left off.

'So why were we not included in this plan?' Gruber said indignantly.

'I really don't know.' Marsden could not bring himself to tell them the Government probably thought they were

41

nothing but a bunch of harmless lunatics.

'Why don't we go and have a look at this plane?' said Campbell.

'Who's going to monitor things here?' asked Benson.

'I'll stay if you like,' volunteered Matthews.

'No need for that, the Professor will be here. I think we should all go.'

'So Ben Hutton is still alive after all,' murmered Marsden.

They all left. The Professor was happily humming and listening, surrounded by sheets of paper covered with crotchets and quavers. He did not even know they had gone.

8

Ben Hutton opened his eyes and put a hand to his aching head. 'Phil,' he called, thinking that his friend must have got out to see where they were. He undid his seat belt and clambered out of the plane. 'My God, that was a close shave,' he thought as he saw just how near the cliff edge he had landed. He straightened up and groaned. 'God, my bones ache, I must be getting old.' He looked about him. There was no sign of Philip. 'Where the Hell am I and where's Philip?' He called again but there was no answer, only a few weird sounds echoed through the trees in the distance. Ben shuddered. 'What on earth is that noise? I'll keep away from that area.'

He walked to the cliff edge and looked over. Some distance away he saw a few people wearing brightly coloured robes trying to climb down the cliff face. 'Stupid idiots,' he thought, 'must be some form of religious sect — but then, who am I to call them stupid, look what we tried to do.' Again, he looked about him as if he would at any minute see Philip coming towards him. 'Expect he's just reconnoitering, trying to find out where we are. But then,' he pondered, 'what difference does it make where we are? We can't get across the Channel now.' He felt a slight tremor under his feet which gathered momentum along the cliff edge until, with a mighty roar, he saw to his horror rocks, earth and boulders spewing down upon the hapless people trying to escape the onslaught.

He heard wild screams as one after another lost their footing. He watched with morbid interest as two figures tried to claw their way to a small ledge just below them but they, too, were engulfed in the landslide and were hurtled through the air to land in the mud and rocks below. Buried alive! Ben felt sick. After the disaster, all was quiet and still as if nothing had happened. 'Why did the landslide have to happen just there?' asked Ben despairingly. 'Had it been further along the cliff, perhaps those people could have escaped. Come to that, there could be another quake any minute and I could be flying through the air.' With that thought he went back to the plane quickly.

'Wish I was more of an engineer – perhaps I could find out what went wrong.' He looked about him again but, of course, there was no sign of Philip. 'While I'm waiting for Phil, might as well have a look at the old crate's ticker.' Ben got out a bag of tools and started to tinker about with the engine. Although he knew very little of the mechanics, as luck would have it he must have inadvertently tightened up the right nut, bolt or piece of wire. He could hardly believe his ears as he heard a throb and a splutter. He left the engines running and walked along the same path as Philip had taken until he reached the edge of the wood. 'Phil,' he called loudly, but again there was only that weird noise which seemed further away now. Ben sighed, unable to believe that Philip had gone off and left him alone in the plane. 'Just goes to show, you never know what a person will do when it comes to the crunch.' He walked sorrowfully back to the plane, got in, bumped along and gradually took off.

'Where the Hell am I going now?' he thought miserably. 'I don't even know what time it is, or what day for that matter. Suppose I'd better make for home. But what good is that? I think I'll just go as far as the old crate will take me. What does it matter if I live or die – there's no-one to care now.' Dejectedly he veered round and headed north-west. He had not gone far when he realised that, once again, something was wrong. 'I'll try and make a better landing this time.' Now that danger loomed, he perked up. Slowly he whirled round over the roof tops of a small village and made a bumpy landing on the top of Berry Hill.

9

Don left the house in a temper. Nora and Robert looked out of the window. 'You'll see, you idiots,' he shouted. 'You'll wish you'd come with me.'

Robert opened the window and yelled, 'Watch out for the dinosaurs, Dad.'

'Don't worry about him, he'll soon be back,' said Nora with a sniff.

'Stupid fairy tales,' muttered Don as he walked smartly out of the gate. He carried a bag over his shoulder in which he had flung a sleeping bag, a bottle of water and a few odds and ends that might come in useful. Soon he was lost to view down the road. Don himself could hardly believe what he was doing – going off and leaving his wife and son, to what?

'I suppose everybody's off their heads with fear these days,' he thought. 'I must have a very strong survival instinct.' With that thought he cheered up and set forth.

On the way he met various stragglers with the same idea as himself – some still soldiering on and some too exhausted to go any further. People were banding together who would never have spoken to each other in the normal way. Once-wealthy businessmen hobnobbing with refuse collectors, cleaning women chatting to bankers' wives. All had only one thing on their minds – to stay alive. The children thought it a great adventure, except those who were sick and had to be carried. After some hours of trekking and sharing the meagre food and water they had brought with them, Don realised they would all have to join forces and go on as a group, helping each other.

'Hi there,' he called to each person he met. 'Let's get together.' And like a Pied Piper he led the way and the people followed him, only too glad for someone to take the lead and organise them. Don did not for one minute think there was anything in the dinosaur story, but on the other hand. . .

There was now a motley crew of some thirty adults and twenty children of varying ages. 'If we are going to survive we must stay together,' said Don. 'We are now on the edge of the forest and we must reach the coast before night.'

They all murmured in acquiescence. Don was beginning to feel quite heady. 'Perhaps I'm a modern Jesus leading my flock across the sea to the promised land,' he thought. This idea gave him added strength as he marched in front of this hopeful crowd.

All of a sudden there was a wild scream from a child who was running in front. They all stood still with fright as they saw a huge beast stampeding through the trees chasing a rabbit. 'So it wasn't a fairy tale after all,' breathed Don. 'Unless we're all lightheaded with lack of food.' He raised his voice and shouted, 'How many people saw that dinosaur?' They all raised their hands. So it must be true.

'Thought dinosaurs only ate leaves?' said one old man.

'This must be a different species,' said a young student who had studied Palaeontology.

'Perhaps they're not man-eating,' ventured another, hopefully.

'I can't go on,' screamed a woman hysterically.

'Shut up, you stupid cow,' said her husband angrily and slapped her on the face. Evidently used to such treatment she went quiet and clung to his arm.

They plodded on looking warily to right and left. One very curious child had lagged behind to look into some bushes where she saw something move. 'Mum,' she shouted, 'look, here's a baby dinosaur.'

Her mother ran back and yanked her along. 'Don't you know if there's a baby one then there's a Mummy and Daddy one too?' she whispered.

'Couldn't I have him for a pet?' the little girl whined.

'No you can't,' she answered, trying to pull the child back.

Too late. There was a loud thrashing of undergrowth and mother dinosaur smashed her huge feet down on them both, crushing the breath out of them.

'Jenny,' shouted a man. He ran back, trying to grab his wife and daughter from the dinosaur's huge claws but was himself struck down and killed instantly.

They were all rooted to the spot with horror and then panic swept through the crowd like a rushing wind. They fled through the forest, picking up the young children as they went. The incident left everyone shaken.

'We must keep together,' shouted Don.

One child cried plaintively, 'Mummy, it's getting dark — I'm afraid.'

'Never mind,' replied her mother, soothingly. 'We'll soon be there,' although she had no idea of where 'there' was. Most were too tired to care where they were going but just followed the crowd like sheep.

After another hour of stumbling and crunching their way through the forest, Don realised that they would have to stop. They came to a clearing where the grass was softer. 'I think we'll have to bed down here for a few hours,' he called.

It was obvious that so many people were exhausted they could hardly walk another step, so they were quite happy for Don to give the orders. It saved having to make any fateful decision. 'I've never come across such a docile lot,' thought Don. 'Surely there must be some aggressive people amongst them?'

So they made their pathetic attempts to settle down for the night. It was beginning to get cold and there were not enough sleeping bags and blankets to go round. People had to huddle together as best they could, eking out the bare rations of food and drink. Don set himself a little apart, sitting on a fallen log, as a leader should — but where were his stalwart henchmen? He looked around his flock. Surely there must be some strong men, or women come to that — mustn't forget the equal rights — who would like to help lead.

Nora was only too happy for him to take the initiative. This thought brought home to him that this was the first time she had ever really disagreed with him. Dammit, it was lonely without her. Supposing she and Robert decided to follow him, they wouldn't know which direction to take; they would get lost. 'I should have made them come with me.' Don was now nearly out of his mind with worry. 'Should I go back?' But then, if they had left and he did not meet them on the way he would be in a worse spot.'At least these people need me. . .' And with that somewhat comforting thought he got out his sleeping bag and, although the ground was hard and all he had was a sweater for a pillow, he managed to sleep soundly till the morning.

He woke to the sounds of those groaning with the discomfort of sleeping on the ground, the coughing and spluttering, and cries of the children. 'Not how it used to be when I went camping,' thought Don. 'Then you got woken up with the screechings of wild fowl, the twittering of birds, the rustlings of rabbits and squirrels leaping about searching for their next meal. Now it seems all you can hope to see is a dinosaur and all these creepy-crawlies that nothing can destroy,' as he shook the insects from his sleeping bag. 'It's a wonder the women aren't screaming – Nora can't stand spiders.'

Sure enough, there was a wild scream but spiders were not the cause of it. A young woman with long hair was standing transfixed to the ground under a tree. In front of her dangled a snake, writhing and hissing. Everyone was standing around open-mouthed, not knowing what to do until suddenly a big Jamaican woman at the back of the crowd pushed her way forward and said to a young man who had brought his guitar along, 'Play something, man.'

'Wh-wh-what shall I play?'

'Anything, you dope.'

The young man took up his guitar and with trembling fingers began to play. The woman swayed to the music and advanced slowly towards the snake. She was a woman of large proportions and her body rippled with every movement. There was a gasp from the crowd as she gently lifted the snake from the branch with slow, rhythmic movements. And, holding the snake above her head, she cried 'Hallelujah' and danced off into the woods.

'My God,' said an old sea captain. 'Haven't seen a show like that since I was in Saigon.'

Everyone was full of admiration for the woman as she calmly walked back to them. 'That was awesome,' said Don. The young girl had fainted and was being revived by her sister.

'Where did you learn to do that?' enquired the young guitarist of the woman.

'Oh, back home in Philadelphia. I belonged to a religious sect who did this as an act of faith in God. First time I ever done it though,' she added with a throaty laugh as she clapped the young guitarist round the shoulders. 'You played good, too, young fellah, else I couldn't have done it.'

There was a round of applause for both of them. 'Anyone would think we'd just been watching a cabaret act,' said one man.

'Yeah,' added another. 'Not used to entertainment this time of the morning.'

After that incident, the group as a whole became closer. With such dangers, who knew what would happen next? They must all rely on each other. After all, you never knew what resources were lying untapped beneath the surface of the most ordinary-looking people. 'So,' thought Don, 'I was wrong about this lot being a docile crowd; in all my days I've never seen anything as courageous as that.'

'I should think we'd better start getting along now,' shouted Don as he once again became the leader. 'We must all keep together.'

They packed up their few belongings and with renewed vigour continued their trek towards the coast. The young girl had now revived and was getting very friendly with the guitarist. 'I suppose there might be one or two romances blossoming along the way,' mused Don as he marched on in front. He was glad that he was still the mainstay of the expedition and he managed to keep them all herded together until they eventually reached that part of the coast where Philip Marsden and Ben Hutton had landed. But now what? They all looked with despair down the cliff face where there had been more landslides and all the mud and slime they would have to go through before reaching the firm sand which had not long ago been the bottom of the Channel.

'I can't go down there,' screamed the hysterical woman.

Her husband slapped her. 'Belt up, you stupid bitch, or I'll leave you behind.'

'Funny she never got hysterical during the snake in-

49

cident,' thought Don. 'Oh well, I suppose Freud would have had an answer for that.'

The poor man was really fond of his wife but did not know how to cope with her hysteria and the last thing he would have done would be to leave her to the mercy of snakes and dinosaurs.

'We must think of some way of getting everyone down the cliff,' said Don in a practical tone.

The old sea captain came forward and drew out of his haversack a very long length of rope. 'Here,' he quavered, 'you can have this, I don't think I'll be able to make it.'

'Come, don't give up now,' coaxed Don. 'We shall need you to tell us whether we're going in the right direction, and also how to tie the damn rope round us.'

That did the trick. Captain Thomsett stood up straight. Even if he was nearly eighty years old, a captain did not desert his crew.

Don knew that many were fearful of making that dangerous descent down the cliff. He looked around at his exhausted crowd. Faint with lack of food, some were just about to collapse. 'Before we do anything else,' he said, 'I think we should pray.' He was surprised at himself. Such a thing had never occurred to him before. But then, he had never come across a life or death situation like this before either.

'You're right,' said the captain. 'That's what we used to do at sea when the storms were bad.'

'I think we should pray to St Christopher,' said another.

'He's the one who keeps you safe on journeys,' chimed in another.

'I think it's best if everyone prays in their own way.'

No sooner had everyone started to offer up their prayers than someone shouted, 'Look,' and pointed to a spot in the distance above the forest which seemed to be coming in their direction. It grew nearer and nearer.

'What is it?'

'Never seen anything like it before.'

'Is it a space ship?'

It was the captain who knew what it was.

'Why, it's a balloon,' he exclaimed.

They all looked up and eventually the balloon came

down very slowly and landed on top of the cliff only a few yards from them. A man got out and shouted to them, 'Are you trying to cross on foot?'

'Yes, what other way is there?' Don shouted back.

The man came up to them. He was an eccentric looking individual, small and thin with a tangled beard, mousey coloured hair, a long nose like a bird which seemed to suit him and was most appropriate to travelling through the air. He was dressed in a black suit which fitted exactly. It seemed as if he only needed a tail. . .

Just then a small child piped up, 'It's the Devil.'

'Hush child,' his mother cried.

Don was annoyed as he did not want to upset the man if there was any chance of help being offered. Luckily the man ignored the remark. 'Look, I'm going back. I've changed my mind. I could take a few people.'

Don looked around at the helpless people all looking at him, relying on him for guidance. How could he leave them defenceless? The Devil man could see his dilemma. 'Why don't you and a few others come and I'll come back for some more,' he offered.

He knew he would not be able to come back but the group did not know this and they seemed reassured. The captain also realised he would not be back but heroically said to Don, 'You go, my boy, and take a few people with you. I'll stay with the others and we'll catch up with you when he comes back for us.'

Don demurred, half guessing the truth of the situation, but allowed the captain to persuade him. 'Come on then, let's sort out who's coming,' said the Devil man, as the children had nicknamed him.

'Who would like to come?' called out Don.

They wavered. Some wanted to go but the husband, wife, girlfriend, boyfriend or child did not want to. Eventually it was decided that the young guitarist and the girl who had been saved from the snake should go as they seemed to be getting on extremely well together. The snake charmer, as she was now called, pushed the couple towards the balloon. 'You go – dat thing won't hold me.'

Then a young mother with a six-year-old girl and three-year-old boy came forward. 'Is that all?' queried Don. He

51

was surprised that so few volunteered. 'It must be the case of the Devil you know.' He smiled at the thought of his own pun. He felt that he was failing in his self-imposed task of leading the tribe into the promised land but on the other hand, if anyone could take over, the captain was the right man. So, reluctantly he helped the chosen ones into the balloon and climbed in himself.

The captain busied himself with the piece of rope and looked about for somewhere to tie it. 'That tree trunk will do.' He went across to a tree trunk which had been struck by lightning. It was near enough to the edge of the cliff for them to tie the rope round and be able to slide down over the edge. He called to two lads who just stood watching. 'Come on lads, help me to fix this rope.'

'That tree ain't strong enough,' remarked one man laconically.

'Got any other ideas then?' replied the captain.

They tied the rope round the tree trunk and hung it over the cliff edge. They could see it fall quite near a gentle slope which they would have to roll down for the last few feet. 'That takes us most of the way down. We only have to navigate the last bit,' said the captain cheerfully.

The nervous woman screamed again as she looked at the rope. The captain took her arm and said reassuringly, 'I think we're just in time, my dear, there's a herd of dinosaurs coming,' and with that remark he fastened the rope round her waist and gently lowered her over the cliff. He knew there had to be a greater fear to make her move.

A few of the younger and more vigorous ones had already gone down the rope and arrived safely at the bottom so they were able to help those who were more at risk. The captain looked round and waved cheerfully to Don. 'See you in France,' he shouted.

The balloon gradually lifted into the air and Don could see the captain waving. They were in good hands. Soon they were lost to view as the balloon moved higher and higher and disappeared.

10

Mary Gruber was sitting in a chair with the cat on her lap, for once not busy. Her neat, tidy world seemed to be falling about her. She could not understand what was going on. She did not really want to understand. She had always taken this line of thought. 'George thinks enough for both of us,' had been her maxim since the day they married. But now things were getting beyond a joke, talking of going to another planet. She feared he had taken leave of his senses. He never talked much about his work and she was quite content just to look after him, the house and the children.

It worried her that there was so little to eat. She was quite happy cooking, washing and keeping house. Life only came to an end when you were old and you died peacefully with your family about you. Any other way of life was unthinkable. Suddenly her reverie was broken into by the telephone ringing. She lifted the cat off her lap, got up slowly and went to answer the phone. She lifted the receiver. 'Hallo, is that you George. . ?'

'No,' a sepulchural voice whispered, 'this is not George. I want to speak to George.'

'He's not here,' Mary did not like the sound of this voice.

'Where is he then?' the voice enquired.

'Who are you?' Mary began to feel uneasy. Perhaps she ought not to say where George was.

'I'm a student of psychic studies and I know your husband is up to something.'

'He's working in his laboratory,' said Mary sharply. 'That's all I know.'

'He's got some formula to fly to another planet, hasn't he?'

'I don't know what you're talking about,' replied Mary angrily. How many more people were going to talk about going to another planet?

'You can't fool me,' the voice went on, a little stronger now. 'He's not going to get away with it.'

'Get away with what?' asked Mary, near to tears.

'It's all right for him with his wonderful plans for going into space and leaving us all behind.'

'What do you mean?' Mary was now becoming quite unnerved by this conversation. Was George in danger from this maniac?

'Don't worry,' the voice continued, 'he's not going anywhere. We'll stop him. . .'

'You leave my George alone. . .'

'I shall now go into meditation. . .' the voice whispered and seemed to trail away. Mary put the phone down. She stood dazed, not knowing what to do. Ought she to warn George? But then he would say she was imagining things.

Just then Katie and Mark burst in. 'Did you hear that noise, Mum?' shouted Mark.

'What noise, dear?'

How nice it was to get back to the normal chatter of her children. 'Perhaps it was some silly person playing a joke,' she thought and dismissed the phone call from her mind. Katie was getting exasperated.

'Didn't you hear it, Mum?'

'It sounded like something coming down out of the sky,' said Mark. 'It made an awful racket.'

'Can we go and have a look?' asked Katie, pleading.

'It might have been a plane,' added Mark.

'But there aren't any planes flying now,' said Mary in a perplexed tone.

'But that's just it. If it wasn't a plane, then what was it?'

'Can we go, Mum?' Katie repeated.

'Where do you think this thing came down?'

'It sounded in the Berry Hill direction,' said Mark.

'Oh, all right then, run along but don't stay out too late.'

Mary looked at them. With all these peculiar things happening she suddenly realised just what these children meant to her. No harm must come to them. 'Be careful. Don't go near anything dangerous.'

They looked at her impatiently. 'It's an adventure,' cried Katie. 'Come on Mark.'

They couldn't wait to run out of the house. Out in the road they saw Robert coming towards them. 'Hi Robert,' called Mark. 'We're going up the hill – you coming?'

Robert joined them and off they ran up the hill to investigate.

It was exhilarating to them to have these exciting things happening. Life was getting boring. All that talk about the end of the world. Religious fanatics were having a field day. But they wanted to live. Perhaps after all, something really exciting was going to happen and somehow their Dad had his finger in the pie too. . .

'That's Dad up there with those men,' shouted Mark, pointing up the hill. 'Come on,' and he raced ahead, leaving Katie and Robert puffing behind him.

Mary had rushed to the door and shouted after them, 'No, don't go. . .'

But they had already gone and did not hear her. The cat miaowed plaintively round her legs. 'Never mind, Timmy, we'll wait for them to come back,' she sighed. 'Why can't things just get back to normal?'

She went back to her chair feeling exhausted and with the cat on her lap she nodded off.

11

Once again Bun Hutton looked about him in a daze. 'Where the Devil am I this time? Must have had another blackout.' He racked his brains trying to remember what had happened. Gradually it came back to him. 'Of course, we never got to France. Landed somewhere on a cliff edge last time.' He eased himself out of the plane to find that again he had been lucky; there were no broken bones. 'Suppose we ran out of juice.'

He looked down the hill and in the distance he could see some figures hurrying towards him. When they got closer he recognised one as Philip. 'Why, the bastard must have left me to rot.' He felt very angry, also his head ached. He could do with a drink of water. Perhaps there might be some left in his bag. A dizziness came over him and he swayed, falling against the wing of the plane.

'Steady on, old man.' Philip, being first on the scene, grabbed his arm. 'Thought you were dead else I'd never have left you like that. I managed to crawl this far and Dr Gruber here found me.'

There were introductions all round. Benson, Campbell and Matthews couldn't wait to have a good look at the plane. 'Manna from Heaven, my boy,' said Gruber, shaking his hand. Ben looked at him stupidly. 'Water,' he gasped.

'Sure, I'll get you some,' said Philip.

He was embarrassed at Ben turning up like this. It made him look a right heel. He climbed into the plane to look for the bottle of water they had taken with them. But how many days was it since they crashed? He could not remember. He found the bottle of water, which smelt foul. Luckily there was an apple which seemed to have a bit of juice in it. He climbed out of the plane and handed the apple to Ben. 'Sorry, this is all I can find for the moment. We can get you some water if you hang on for a bit.'

The others were engrossed in examining the plane.

'Look at that instrument panel,' said Benson.

'It's really antique, isn't it?' replied Campbell.

'Who cares? It might be more simple to adapt.'

'We may not have to adapt. We can simply disregard it and use our own equipment.'

Matthews was trying to assess how many people the plane would hold if they were all crammed together. Gruber was still surveying the outside. Even he was beginning to think that perhaps the whole idea was utterly absurd. 'What's going on?' asked Ben weakly.

'Dr Gruber's got some tremendous idea of using sound waves to get to another planet,' said Philip nonchalantly.

'Good God!'

'There's nothing else left. Our last hope was getting to France for the airbus.' Philip thought he would just let Ben think that he would have been included in that escape plan. After all, this time he would be able to go with them.

'How many do you think we can squeeze into this plane?' asked Gruber.

Ben thought for a minute. 'It's only an eight-seater really, my father only used it for his business conferences.'

The others climbed out of the plane, brimming with hope and excitement. Matthews came out first. 'Reckon we could get about twelve on it. Perhaps more if children could sit on their parents' laps.'

'If you can get the lift off,' said Philip, 'how long do you think it will take to get to this new planet?'

'Difficult to say,' replied Gruber. 'It may not take time as we know it. Of course, we won't be able to test out our theory first.'

'Kill or cure, I suppose?'

'Of course, time will be different on another planet,' added Benson. 'It could have longer or shorter days.'

'Suppose we arrive somewhere else in the galaxy?' asked Campbell.

Gruber frowned. 'That couldn't happen, either we arrive on planet X or we disappear into space.'

'I was going to say,' said Benson, 'it could also depend upon the shape of the planet.'

'Aren't they all like the Earth, only bigger or smaller?' asked Ben.

Matthews replied in a jocular tone, 'I shouldn't think we're likely to find a square or triangular planet.'

'But supposing there are other planets with the same sound as planet X,' continued Campbell, 'and the same shape?'

'Most unlikely,' said Gruber, not interested in the turn their thoughts were taking. He was the eternal optimist. To him it was quite pointless and a complete waste of time to consider ifs and buts.

'If there were,' added Matthews, 'we would be flying around like a blue-assed fly in perpetual motion and not getting anywhere.'

'Or maybe it could give us more than one opportunity,' suggested Benson.

'That's a bit more positive,' said Gruber, nodding his head. They continued debating amongst themselves about the pros and cons of their outrageous ideas until there was a shout of 'Daddy', and they saw Katie, Mark and Robert running up the hill towards them. All three fell on the ground completely out of breath. The men were not amused. This was not the time to have kids skylarking around. Serious thinking and planning had to be done, and soon. Also, it would be dark in a few hours. 'But,' thought Benson, 'it might be better to work in the dark, then other children and students wouldn't know what was going on. Better keep these kids quiet.' They couldn't take the whole community and he knew some people would rather set the plane on fire than let a few have the chance of another life.

'Come and have a look inside,' he cajoled.

They didn't need asking twice. 'Can we?' they were over-awed.

'You'll have to keep it a real secret,' said Benson.

'Can't we tell Mummy?' asked Mark.

'A secret is something you can't tell anyone,' he repeated.

'O.K.' They all agreed to keep quiet.

'Let's get in then,' said Robert eagerly. 'My Dad will miss this, he's gone off to North Africa.'

Everyone pricked up their ears at this remark. 'You mean he's gone off and left you? What about your mother?' asked Gruber.

'She's gone round to see Mrs Gruber,' he said, climbing after Robert into the plane.

'Poor sod,' they all thought. 'Gone off his rocker. Hasn't got a chance.'

'I guess he felt he couldn't just sit around and do nothing,' said Campbell.

'He needn't have left his wife and kid behind,' added Benson.

'Well, each to their own. We must get back to the lab,' said Gruber. He was sorry about Don but there was no time for sympathy. 'Why don't you, Marsden and your friend Ben go back to my home and you can take the kids with you when they've satisfied their curiosity?'

Gruber looked at the two men, thinking neither of them could help in the delicate work they had to do and would only clutter up the lab. This was agreed and he strode off followed by Benson, Campbell and Matthews.

'The Professor has probably got something worked out by now,' said Gruber confidently.

'Unless he's still asleep,' joked Campbell.

'Or shot himself into space,' added Matthews.

'We'll have to think of a name for this planet,' said Benson, changing the subject. He knew Gruber would get annoyed at these teasing remarks as he could not understand negative humour. 'Any ideas?' he threw out as they hurried down the hill.

'As it's the Earth's opposite, why not turn the letters the other way round?'

'Not possible. You could only use the letters in a different way.'

'Like Retah, you mean?'

'You don't usually name something until you've seen it,' remarked Matthews.

'What a philosophical chap you are,' said Benson. 'After all, what's in a name. . ?'

59

12

The balloon was more than half way across the Channel and the occupants were beginning to feel really cold. There seemed to be a gale force wind coming up to which the young guitarist and his girlfriend were quite oblivious. Completely wrapped up in themselves, all these dangerous exploits they had been through brought them closer together.

'I don't even know your name, mine's Kevin.'

'Linda,' she said softly.

'Lovely name,' he looked at her fondly.

The Devil man, although he had been obliging enough to take them across, had now withdrawn into himself and seemed completely remote, acting as if they were not even there.

'I expect he's fed up with all that billing and cooing,' Don thought, looking at the young couple. He felt uneasy and tried to reassure the young woman, Jessie, and her two children that they would soon be in France. He did not like to admit that he was terrified. But maybe if the wind was going in the right direction it would get them there faster, or not at all.

The children couldn't stand this silence any longer and the little girl piped up, 'Mummy, is the Devil man taking us to Hell?' Little Jimmy stared at her and clung tighter to his mother and bedraggled teddy bear.

Jessie looked embarrassed and said, 'Sssh, Angie, this kind man is rescuing us from the dinosaurs, don't you remember?'

'Oh yes,' said Angie and turned to their rescuer. 'Mr Devil man, what is your real name?'

He seemed to come back into the land of the living, looked at the child and with a smile said, 'My name is Hercules.'

There didn't seem to be any answer to that. A more incongruous name for this little man his parents could never have found.

Linda and Kevin had been whispering quietly until Kevin suddenly said in a loud voice, 'Are you like the captain of a ship, Hercules? Could you marry us?'

'How romantic,' exclaimed Jessie.

Don thought, 'How ridiculous. Here they were being buffeted about by the wind and now the rain was lashing them as well.'

'Sorry, young man,' replied Hercules, 'I don't have that authority.'

'You'll have to wait for the sea captain to catch us up,' said Don, knowing it to be an impossibility.

'I never thought of him,' said Kevin putting a protective arm around Linda. 'What a pity we didn't think of that before.'

'Bit of a gale blowing up, isn't there?' said Don apprehensively.

They seemed to be flying through the air as if jet-propelled, and with the wind buffeting them to and fro it was as much as they could do to grip the sides of the basket. The children were screaming with fright when the storm blew away as suddenly as it had come, but it was an uneasy calm.

Looking up, Don saw a pigeon circling round the balloon. As it came nearer he could see it had something in its beak. Hercules got hold of a long pair of tweezers and took the object from the bird. Jessie and the children watched in amazement as Hercules unwrapped a small scroll, read it and tossed it away.

'What was that, Mummy?' said Angie, always inquisitive.

'I don't know, it must have been a message,' she replied.

Don was thinking that they had no clue to this man's identity. Who was he, where had he come from and, more importantly, where was he going? Did he belong to the Secret Service?

Hercules was also wondering whether he should tell

61

these good people who he was. It was unlikely now that he would be able to catch the airbus to America as they had changed the take-off venue, which was to have been the old Charles de Gaulle airport. Now it was Brussels airport. Even if he could navigate the balloon in that direction, what was he going to do with these people? He had intended landing near Paris and leaving them to fend for themselves on their way south. 'Perhaps I could pass them all off as my family,' he wondered.

His story, of course, was much the same as Philip Marsden's. He had been a loner for a number of years and worked at the same type of nuclear plant in Hampshire. His hobby had been pigeon fancying – so what better way could there be to send a message to Paris to say he had found a method of getting there. They in turn had sent the pigeon back to him saying the airport in France was waterlogged and take-off would be from Brussels and would be delayed for a further day. Three weeks earlier he had received a message through the computer that the flight had been put off and to await further directions. All those, like Philip Marsden, who had gone rushing off were not aware of this. 'I was mad to get lumbered with these people,' he thought. 'Why on earth didn't I keep going on my own?'

'I'm afraid I won't be able to drop you off in Paris after all,' he said apologetically. 'I have to try and get to Brussels.'

'That's the world nuclear centre, isn't it?' asked Don.

'What's the use?' thought Hercules. 'What does it matter if I tell him,' and like Marsden he thought it was too late to bother about secrets.

'There's an airbus going off from Brussels early tomorrow morning. From there we are supposed to go to America and get the lift off to the Shangri-la Space Station.'

'Good God,' exclaimed Don. 'So I presume the Government thinks there is absolutely no hope for anyone?'

'That's about it.'

'Well I'm damned. So old Gruber was right after all. Perhaps I should have listened to him instead of thinking he was a bloody madman.'

'And who is Gruber, may I ask?'

'A scientist who lived next door to us. He said he had found a way of getting to another planet.'

'Sounds interesting.'

'It probably was. We just thought he was mad and took no notice of his crazy ideas.'

'I wish I could have met him.'

'Yes, I wonder what he's up to now. . . I suppose there's no chance any of us could get on this airbus?'

'I'm afraid not, but I did wonder,' Hercules looked at Jessie, 'if I could pass off Jessie here as my wife. That is, if she wants to take such a risk.'

'Nothing ventured, nothing gained,' she replied.

The two lovebirds were completely oblivious to this conversation.

'That's the true pioneer spirit. You're just the sort of person we shall need,' Hercules said as he looked at Jessie admiringly. 'Maybe it might not be such a bad idea at that,' he thought.

Jessie merely thought that at this stage of events there was certainly nothing to lose.

'What about me?' said Don anxiously.

Hercules looked at him with a frown. What indeed?

Angie whispered to little Jimmy. 'I think the Devil man is going to be our Dad.' He clung to his mother more tightly.

'Look,' shouted Jessie. Sure enough, through a gap in the clouds they could see buildings. 'Is that France?'

'I don't think so,' said Hercules. 'Well I'm damned. That terrible gale has blown us across to Belgium, just where I wanted to get to after all.'

He pointed. 'There's the Atomium. I'll try and find a good place to land.'

He could see the airport and gradually they came down and landed firmly on a piece of waste ground only a short distance from the airport. They all tumbled out of the basket, their legs weak with not being able to move and general exhaustion with lack of food and water. They looked around and nearby saw a disused café. Luckily the door was open so they crept in.

'What a horrible smell,' said Angie disdainfully.

'Never mind that,' said Jessie. 'Is there anything fit to eat?'

'And drink,' added Hercules.

Don turned on the tap and water spurted out. 'Thank

God we've got water.'

'And here's some tins of food,' said Jessie as she looked on the shelves. 'I can make us a meal out of some of these.' So she set to and in no time she managed to make a meal of sorts. They were so hungry they didn't care what they ate. Linda, who had once been so fussy about her food, sat down and ate the beans and soup with gusto.

After partaking of this sumptuous repast, Hercules said they must press on and get to the airport. The children were tired now and wanted to rest, but he insisted.

'I'll carry the little one,' he said.

Linda and Kevin said they would try and make their own way. They said their thank-yous and goodbyes and walked off arm in arm down the road towards. . . where?

'Poor young things,' thought Hercules.

'Is there any chance I could get back to Berry Hill in your balloon?' asked Don.

He was suddenly homesick. He knew there was no chance for him to get on the airbus and if Hercules managed to get Jessie and the children on then he would be left entirely alone and the only alternative would be to wait for the others he had left trekking across the Channel.

Hercules looked surprised. 'You might just make it,' he sounded relieved. 'Although there's not much time to give you instruction.'

'I've been taking note of what you were doing and anyway I know there's no hope for me so I think I'll just try and get back to my wife and son. I should never have left them in the first place.' Don realised now how much he missed them.

'Well, if that's how you feel. . .'

'It is and if I kill myself in the process it really won't matter very much.'

'O.K. Then I'll get you started off. Come on.'

They hurried back to the balloon. Jessie and the children followed slowly. With the briefest of instructions Hercules explained how to take off and land. 'It'll be a miracle if you get back,' he couldn't help saying.

'Leave it to fate then,' said Don matter of factly.

He looked across at Jessie and shouted, 'Hope you make it.'

Jessie was too choked to speak and just waved.

Don saw Hercules pick up Jimmy and Angie take her mother's hand. They all waved as he wafted away.

'Where's he going?' enquired Angie.

'Up to Heaven I should think,' replied Jessie.

13

Back at the laboratory the Professor was waiting for them. 'I need a harp,' he cried, 'and a female soprano.'

They looked non-plussed. They could soon get the harp from Gruber's house, but a soprano? It would mean asking one of their students and then no longer could they keep their secret.

'Is it a female planet, then?' asked Benson.

For once the Professor aired his opinion. 'Not necessarily. It might be some form of mating tone.'

'If everything goes by opposites,' said Gruber, 'as our planet is female then planet X must be male.'

'Or vice versa,' suggested Matthews.

'While you're cogitating on that, we'll go and get the harp,' said Campbell.

'What about Vikki's voice?' suggested Matthews.

'Or young Katie,' added Campbell.

'Good idea. Bring them along too,' said Gruber.

'Come to that,' said Benson, 'does it have to be a female? What about Robert? His voice hasn't broken yet.'

'Perhaps that could work,' said the Professor weakly. He was feeling really tired now and would really like to have a little nap.

Benson could see how exhausted the old man was. 'Why don't you have a rest, Professor? There's a couch in the room next door, why not have forty winks?'

'Good idea.' The Professor followed Benson into the next room.

'Try and find Robert as well then,' said Gruber to Campbell.

Campbell and Matthews left hurriedly. They were all

aware now of the mounting tension as Gruber's invention seemed to be literally getting off the ground. Gruber went back to studying the screen with Benson who was desperate to get on with his new ideas about shape.

'Let's fix up the graph locater,' suggested Benson.

The locater was on the wall beside the computer. Gruber found its connecting wires and plugged them into the back of the computer. Immediately dots and dashes were flying about all over the place on the locater.

'These sounds seem to be zig-zagging in all different directions,' said Gruber.

'Perhaps that has something to do with the shape,' said Benson excitedly.

He pressed the button to operate the printout. 'Look.' Gruber pointed as fine lines began to appear. 'Looks like a beehive.'

Very gradually the drawing began to take shape as they waited with bated breath. 'Looks like a pair of kidneys,' said Benson, 'or is it a heart?'

'Or voice box,' added Gruber.

'Or magnetic field.'

They looked at each other, the light dawning. As more lines began to appear Benson said, 'There are so many things this could be, look – now it's the sex organs.'

'Now a bee in flight,' added Gruber.

'And now it looks like a brain,' said Benson.

'Maybe we tuned into the Big Brain,' Gruber's voice went quite hoarse.

'Perhaps this is the ultimate shape,' said Benson as the locater seemed to be slowing down.

'Perhaps I'd better wake up the Professor now.' Just as Gruber said the words the Professor came in.

'How can a man take a nap with you two shouting your heads off?' he said grumpily.

'Just look at this,' said Benson soothingly.

'Gordon Bennett,' exclaimed the Professor. 'What have you found?'

'I think we've found the shape of the universe,' said Gruber.

'We may have touched on the origins of the blueprint of the universe – maybe it's just one big enormous brain,' added Benson.

The locater was still moving but more slowly. More and more fine lines kept appearing but these were only making the one shape more intricate.

'Have you noticed, Benson,' said Gruber, 'there are no straight lines, they are all curved?'

'So they are – look now.'

'One can see so many different things in the shape. Now there are not only lines but dots as well coming in.'

All three watched fascinated at the beautiful drawing being woven by the locater.

'This is more than we could have hoped for, isn't it?' Gruber rubbed his hands gleefully.

'Now we have sound and shape,' said Benson, 'I wonder if there's anything else.'

'It must have some sort of positive charge,' replied Gruber.

The Professor was dumbfounded by this quick interchange of ideas. He tended to work slowly and methodically – not darting about all over the place with these incredible thoughts.

'Yes, everything has to have friction.'

Gruber pondered for a moment. 'Then again, is space travel only going to succeed if we have a vehicle in this particular shape?'

'Well, I suppose you could say a plane is fairly similar, with the main body and the two wings.'

'Brilliant,' said Gruber.

'And I suppose,' the Professor at last managed to get a word in, 'this is where the voice comes in also, the voice apparatus being the same shape.'

Awareness of each others thoughts heightened. The inspiration issuing forth was like an electric charge in the room. Excitement mounted. Perhaps it was just as well they had been left to their own devices. They could press on without any Government interference. There was no-one to come muscling in to seize their invention, work on it somewhere else and then leave the inventors behind.

'Yehooo,' shouted Benson, totally out of character. 'If music be the food of travel, play on. . .' and he snatched a piece of the Professor's music and started waving it about.

Gruber did not have much sense of humour and to him this was procrastination. 'Let's get on, I think it's going to be very complicated and time is running out. The main idea is simple but the workings are like the inside of a computer.'

'Surely, the main thing is to try and imitate the workings of the brain?' said Benson.

'Easier said than done,' added the Professor. He was now beginning to feel more in the swing of things.

'Don't be pessimistic – just think what an impact music has on the brain.' Gruber could not tolerate the way people would keep putting spokes in the wheel.

'I was going to say,' said the Professor, 'maybe the reason it needs a string instrument like the harp as a basis is because it ripples.'

Benson, although not much of a musician, could see this. 'And then the sounds can be moulded into the shape.'

'Look,' Gruber pointed to the screen which was still bleeping, 'the locater seems to have stopped.'

'At least that must mean there is an end to the universe,' queried the Professor.

'I hadn't thought of that.' Gruber was entranced with this point of view.

'Getting back to the shape,' said Benson, 'this music will have to be put in a receptacle which is also the shape of the brain.'

'Do you think a plane is going to be near enough?' asked Gruber. How many more obstacles were going to be put in the way?

'No,' Benson was exasperated, 'I mean a receptacle to put into the plane.'

'Oh.' Gruber could now see what Benson was driving at. 'Obviously everything has to follow through on the same theme.'

'Exactly. What the Hell are we going to use?'

'Don't panic,' said the Professor calmly. 'We've got so far, the answer must be around us somewhere.'

Benson was far from panicking. He was in deep thought. 'What about one of those antique recording machines they used to use years ago?'

'You mean with two spools which you could wind backwards and forwards?' queried Gruber.

'That's it. There's an old junk cupboard in the room next door with all sorts of stuff in it. I remember Mary was going to throw it away so I brought it here for safe keeping.'

For once, thought Benson, perhaps I shall be glad that Gruber is a hoarder. 'Let's go and look.'

'Right-e-oh,' agreed Gruber.

The Professor went back to his notes, happy that these two brilliant men seemed to be cracking the problem.

14

Mary Gruber woke up with a start at the sound of a loud knock at the door. Thinking the children had come back early, she hurried to open it. But it was Nora, near to tears.

'Oh Mary,' she said, and the tears started to flow.

'What's the matter, dear? Come in and sit down.'

Mary was only too glad to have someone to talk to who wasn't in the clouds. She led Nora into the sitting room and made her sit down. 'Sit down dear and tell me all about it.'

She spoke as if to a child. 'What a pity I can't offer her a cup of tea,' she thought. 'Nothing seems so bad after a nice cup of tea.' But there was only a little tea left so she thought she had better wait and see just how bad the news was before using it up. After all, something much worse might happen.

'He's gone,' whimpered Nora.

'Gone where?'

'I don't know. . . he said he was going to try and get to North Africa.'

'What on earth is going on? Has everyone gone mad?'

'He said if we didn't go with him he would go on his own and he just stormed off down the road,' Nora choked.

'What about Robert?'

'He didn't want to go. He said he would rather stay here. He's gone off with Mark and Katie. They went to look at some old plane that's landed on the hill.'

Nora felt slightly better at the thought that at least Robert hadn't deserted her as well.

'The children did rush off to look at something,' Mary sighed. 'I wasn't really listening.'

Mary had put her head in the sand for so long, and not

really listened to anything that was being said, that she was now groping in the dark.

'Everything's getting so bad, Don said unless we get away from here we just won't survive.'

'What nonsense,' said Mary weakly. 'Where could we go?'

'That's what I say,' agreed Nora.

For once they were together in their fear. How could their normal easy-going life be upset like this? They were both immersed in their own thoughts when there was a loud knock at the door. 'Who's that?' Nora jumped up, her heart in her mouth. Could it be Don – had he come back? Maybe a few hours of walking had cooled him off, and now he realised what he had done.

Mary also got up quickly and went to the door. Matthews and Campbell rushed in. 'We've come for the harp,' said Campbell. 'Got to hurry.' They grabbed the harp from the corner of the room. 'Heave ho. . .'

Together they lifted the harp and were out of the house before either of the two women could say anything. 'Have you seen. . ?' began Nora, but the door slammed before she could even ask them if they had seen Don.

'Am I dreaming?' asked Mary.

'If you are, then so am I,' replied Nora.

'I'm beginning to feel as if I'm in a sort of Alice in Wonderland.'

Just as Mary spoke there was another knock at the door. Nora opened it. Campbell rushed in again. 'Where are Katie and Robert?'

'They went out – and Mark as well,' said Mary.

'They went up the hill to look at the plane – they haven't come back yet,' added Nora.

'Damn,' said Campbell. 'We need them. Will you ask them to come straight round to the laboratory when they come in?' He rushed out again like a whirlwind, leaving Mary and Nora speechless.

'Well I never,' was all Mary could manage.

Nora felt alarmed. What could scientists want with a couple of kids? Before she had time to speak, Campbell rushed in again.

'Can I use your phone? I must phone Vikki.'

Mary waved her hand towards the phone. 'Go ahead.'

Campbell dialled the number of their apartment. He waited impatiently for her to answer.

'Vikki, come over to the lab now. Leave everything. Just come now.' He slammed the phone down. Before he could rush out again Nora grabbed his arm.

'What's going on, why do you want my Robert?'

'Can't explain now,' he replied, breaking away from her grasp. 'We may know soon. Don't worry. There may be a chance. Don't be frightened. Just stay here.'

Before she could say any more, Campbell ran up the path to join Matthews who was waiting impatiently with the harp.

Nora looked out of the window. 'Matthews looks as if he's ready for the next world now,' she said cryptically.

Mary joined her at the window and they watched as Campbell helped to lift the harp and they staggered off down the road towards the laboratory. It had only just dawned on Mary that they also wanted Katie. 'How can children help with their wretched experiments?'

Mary was feeling very irritable. She did not really mind what her husband got up to in that sacred laboratory of his, but involving the children was another matter. 'Come to that,' she said aloud, 'why did they not mention Mark? Why only Katie and Robert?'

'It's beyond me,' agreed Nora. 'I don't understand all this technical stuff.'

'But a harp isn't technical.'

'No, that's music.'

They looked at each other in bewilderment, both feeling lost and helpless. 'Should we let them go, do you think?' Mary felt full of misgivings at the thought of Katie being allowed into the laboratory. 'But surely George wouldn't take any chances with his little girl?' she thought, and was relieved to hear Nora saying, 'Well, I shouldn't think it could be anything actively dangerous.'

Nora was merely trying to put Mary's mind at ease. She herself was not so sure. The whole thing sounded very peculiar.

'Oh well,' said Mary in a more optimistic tone, 'I expect it's a lot of excitement about nothing. I'm used to George's experiments, you know. Just a lot of hot air, like his other

73

experiments. I think we should take no notice of it at all. You'll see, everything will be back to normal soon.'

Nora looked at her but this time did not agree.

15

Don had mixed feelings up there in the balloon by himself. 'Am I a fool to try and get back?' he thought. 'Perhaps Nora won't want me now anyway. After all, I was a bastard to go off like that.' There was a fairly strong wind and the air felt a little warmer. 'At least it's stopped raining. I wonder how those poor sods are getting on trying to walk across. What an idiot I was to think of walking to North Africa.'

He looked down but it was too misty to see anything or anybody. In fact, really he was glad he couldn't see them. He could imagine the old captain heroically trying to keep going, trying to spur them on. Those who were not fit would drag themselves along until they dropped with exhaustion. He had a momentary feeling of wanting to find them and take the lead again. It was the first time in his life he had ever felt power – the power to lead others.

'Perhaps I should have been a politician,' he mused. 'I wouldn't have gone off to some cushy hideout up there.' He looked up into the clouds. 'I would have tried to lead the people to safety before it was too late.' He seemed to be borne along with these noble thoughts. Why was it that now it was too late, he knew what his role in life was meant to be? But perhaps it was not too late. His pulse quickened. Supposing Dr Gruber could get them to another planet, would they not want a leader? Those scientists lived in another world all the time – they would need a man, a practical man, with leadership qualities to guide them.

'I should have stayed behind after all but then I suppose if I had then I would never have known about my true role in life. Yes, that's what I must do, get back and lead my flock into the new world.' He was much cheered by these thoughts and of all the noble deeds he was capable of. 'But then, what about Nora? Perhaps she will tell me to get lost. Maybe she won't have me back. Or maybe there won't be room for me or,' he felt panic overcoming him, 'perhaps they will have gone already by the time I get back. I seem to have lost all sense of time.'

There was a faint red glow in the sky. 'It must be nearly sunset,' he thought. 'Oh God, let me be in time. I won't be able to see anything if it gets dark.' Then through the misty haze he saw a few tree tops. 'I'll just have to guess the right direction.' Puffing merrily along he saw one or two landmarks he recognised. There was the cathedral they had toured around and that eighteenth century pub they had stayed in one weekend. He reminisced about the places where they had been. What good times they used to have. Must be getting near Berry Hill now, surely? Soon it would be too dark to see anything.

He peered down. It was difficult to see through the mist that was swirling round him. 'What if I landed amongst those dinosaurs? Supposing they were to reach Berry Hill? After all, they were big creatures. They could cover a lot of ground in a short time.' And so his mind ran on, re-miniscing about the past, then reliving the past few hours. How long had he been away? He began to feel dizzy. 'Pull yourself together, man. You can't faint now, not after all you've been through. I must keep my mind active. I wonder what happened to the young lovers – I hope they make it to their garden of Eden. And the poor old sea captain and the neurotic woman – I suppose I'll never know what happened to them all.'

So he kept himself awake floating through the clouds. He felt desperately alone. He only wanted to be back with his wife and son and the people he knew. 'I don't care now if I get away or not – what does it matter? I think I've had enough adventure. I just want to see them all again. God, what's that?' There was a terrible clap of thunder. He shivered. 'Sounds like guns but it can't be, there isn't any Army now.' Then a fork of lightning streaked across the sky. 'Oh no, it's a storm. That's all I need now. I shall probably land in the top of a tree and blow myself up in this thing.'

76

His eyes suddenly lit up. 'Of course, didn't the Devil man say there was a parachute in case of emergency? Don't despair, man. Here's the parachute in this box.' He got the parachute out and with trembling fingers managed to fix it on himself. He looked down and could only see trees. 'I'll never be able to land, I'll just have to jump and hope for the best. Never did like heights very much at the best of times.' Just as there was another clap of thunder he saw a patch of land between the trees. 'It's now or never. No. . . I can't do it.' He had a dialogue with himself, thinking up all the excuses he could for not jumping. Then suddenly he realised he was running out of gas. 'Well, that's it. Here goes.'

He clung to the edge of the basket and then let go.

16

The children soon got bored with looking at the plane, although Robert was the most interested, almost as if he knew he was going to be involved in this experiment. 'Come on Rob,' shouted Mark. 'We're going.'

Katie was already running down the hill. She looked back. 'Race you.' That was enough for Mark and Robert. Off they went like whirlwinds. Whatever happened, Katie must not be allowed to get home first.

'Where do these kids get their energy from?' asked Hutton, who was still feeling pretty drowsy.

'Don't ask me,' replied Marsden. 'They never get a good meal inside them,' and he let his mind dwell once again on the super food he would now be eating if only he hadn't missed the airbus. Hutton interrupted these thoughts of gastronomic delights.

'What are those three guys up to?'

Marsden had forgotten that Hutton did not have the vaguest idea of what the scientists had in mind. 'As far as I can make out, Gruber, who seems to be the head of the outfit, has hit on some scheme for reaching another planet through sound waves.'

'That sounds great, but how does it work? You can't sit on a sound wave and go roaring up into space.'

'Too true,' agreed Marsden. 'They're thinking of using your plane.'

Hutton stopped in his tracks. 'What?' He could not believe his ears. Was he dreaming? Had Marsden really said that?

'I know it sounds mad,' continued Marsden, 'but that is the absolute truth.'

'Shitty death,' exclaimed Hutton and then laughed uproariously. 'Go into space in my Dad's old plane?' The idea was so preposterous he laughed again.

Marsden looked at him with some sympathy. 'Good old down to earth Ben,' he thought.

'All the same,' he said aloud, 'there might be something in it. I was in the laboratory when they were talking about it.'

Hutton gaped. He became silent and looked at Marsden in consternation. 'Do you mean you really go along with that crazy notion?'

'Well. . . when you think of it, what else is there to go along with?'

'Hmm. . .' Hutton was now subdued. He did realise that their time was limited but this seemed to be the very last straw. On the other hand, could that crazy chap be right? Had he hit on some universal law of interplanetary travel? Marsden broke in on his thoughts.

'After all, when you think of it, electricity was here all the time — it only needed someone to discover it. Perhaps it's the same with sound waves.'

'Maybe. . . Hey, where are those kids?'

They had been so engrossed in their conversation they had not noticed the children were now out of sight.

'Do you know the way back to Gruber's house?' Hutton remarked nervously.

'He lives quite near the laboratory. We should be able to find it all right,' said Marsden quite calmly.

The air was heavy with approaching dusk and the half dead trees had a skeletal look about them. Marsden shivered. The branches seemed like claws ready to suck the life out of anything that came near. There were no birds left to trill in leafy branches. Just the crunch, crunch of their feet as they trudged along. Suddenly there was a weird noise in the distance breaking the torpid stillness. 'What the Hell's that?' Hutton exclaimed.

'God knows,' replied Marsden. 'Whatever it is I don't like the sound of it.'

'Reminds me of those noises you used to hear at the zoo,' said Hutton reminiscently.

'But there are no zoos now.'

They looked at each other in fear. 'Do you think some of those animals are still alive?'

'I don't want to find out. Come on. Perhaps we can catch up with those kids.'

Marsden started walking faster. Hutton had a job to keep up with him. Eventually they came to a lane which branched off. 'I don't recognise this. We must have gone wrong somewhere.'

Hutton had no idea where he was. 'It'll be dark soon. We won't be able to see where we're going.'

'Well, shall we turn right or left?'

'Wouldn't it be better to go back to the plane?' suggested Hutton. 'After all, we can't do anything.'

'That's right. It's Gruber's baby – he's not going to listen to anything we might have to say.'

'Listen,' Hutton said quickly, 'I can hear another noise.'

'Sounds like a football match in the distance,' said Marsden with a frown. 'I know,' he suddenly realised, 'it's the students. I reckon they've got wind of something. In which case they'll be after Gruber and Co like a pack of wolf hounds.'

'What's that?' Hutton spun round and looked towards a clump of trees. It was the beginning of an area which had once been full of unusual flowers, plants and shrubs. A shadow seemed to pass through the trees. 'Did I see something?' Hutton was trying to peer into the depths of the trees.

'Looked a bit like a big brown cat,' volunteered Marsden.

Hutton quaked. 'A bit cat? That could be a lion!'

Then again came that terrible roar. Much closer this time. 'That's not a lion,' said Marsden, feeling just as nervous but trying not to show it. 'Come on, let's get back to the plane.' So they began to retrace their steps.

Hutton stood still. 'I can hear a splashing noise now.'

No sooner had he spoken than they came upon a stream and, to their disbelief, there was a baby dinosaur who appeared to be taking a bath, splashing merrily and luckily completely unaware of the intruders. Suddenly, a bat flew out of a tree round Marsden's head. He yelled, 'Look out,' to Hutton. This sudden noise brought forth a mighty roar from two dinosaurs who were looking for their baby on the other side of the stream. Marsden and Hutton fled for their lives as they heard the threshing and flailing of enormous feet trampling the undergrowth behind them. Any bush or tree that got in the way of the dinosaurs was flattened by them in their rage.

'Can't go on,' puffed Hutton.

Just as he was slowing down he stumbled over a tree root and fell. Marsden looked back and saw Hutton crumpled on the ground. Just then there was a crack of thunder and lightning streaked across the sky. He raced back to Hutton and propped him up against the tree trunk. The dinosaurs stopped in their tracks and after another crack of thunder followed by forked lightning they considered the chase was not worthwhile, turned and stomped off.

'Are you O.K. Ben?'

Hutton stood up weakly. 'Yes, I'm all right.'

'It'll certainly be fate if we survive this lot. If we're not trampled on by dinosaurs we'll probably be struck by lightning.'

'But you know what's odd, Phil. . ?'

'Everything seems odd at the moment.'

'Yes, I know, but it hasn't rained.'

'Well, it may be odd but at least it's one calamity less to put up with. It certainly frightened off the dinosaurs. D'you think you can manage to press on now?'

'Yes, we must soldier on,' said Hutton valiantly.

The thunder died down and there was no more lightning. They plodded on, looking around for signs of life. There were none.

17

Campbell and Matthews carried the harp into the laboratory. The professor was overjoyed. Now he could get on. He couldn't wait to sit down and try out the music he had composed. His eyes gleamed with anticipation. How wonderful to be in on something like this, he thought, when only a little while ago he had been wrapped in a blanket shrivelling into a gradual decline with no hope. His fingers twitched in anticipation.

'Hold on Professor, let's get it onto the floor first.' Campbell could see how overjoyed the Professor was. They carefully set it beside the Professor.

'Off you go now.'

The Professor lovingly strummed his bony fingers along the harp. 'Marvellous instrument,' added Matthews, who had never been very interested in music.

Campbell looked round. 'Where are Gruber and Benson?'

He wondered if he was missing out on something.

'Only next door looking for a tape recorder,' said the Professor.

Just then, Gruber and Benson came in, Benson carrying an antiquated old tape recorder. 'Anyone got a duster?' he enquired hopefully as he blew thirty years of dust off it.

The Professor extracted a handkerchief from his pocket. 'Here, use this.'

Benson managed to open the lid and sure enough there were the two spools with plenty of unused tape. 'It's not so dusty inside,' he said. They were all intrigued.

'It's an old fashioned tape recorder,' Benson told them as he plugged it into a spare socket on the wall.

'Play something, Professor, and we'll soon see if it works,' said Gruber. He was delighted that something he had kept for so long, which had incidentally belonged to his father, should have come in useful at such a time, especially as his wife was always throwing things away. 'Thank God I brought it here,' he thought, 'otherwise it would have been put in the rubbish bin. Well, fate does work in mysterious ways.'

'Why can't we use a modern machine?' enquired Campbell.

'Of course, you two weren't here,' said Benson.

'We've missed something, haven't we?' Campbell said petulantly. 'I thought so.'

'Don't get uptight, Campbell, we'll fill you in on it. Just keep quiet, everybody, for the moment,' said Gruber. He had no patience with jealous squabbles. 'Every sound in this room will come out on the tape.'

The Professor twanged away and Gruber turned on the machine. 'Ssshh. . .'

'O.K. that will do. Now we'll run it back.' Gruber's hands were trembling.

He reversed the tape and then started the playback.

They were all amazed at the beautiful tones of the harp.

'Is that the music of planet X?' asked Benson.

'Oh no,' said the Professor. 'I wouldn't try that just yet. Better make sure the thing works first.'

'Yes, yes,' said Gruber impatiently. 'It does work, doesn't it, much better than I thought it would. My father used to use this tape, you know. Something to be said for the old fashioned things after all.'

Benson then realised that Campbell and Matthews had only brought the harp with them. 'Did you not find Katie and Robert?'

'And Vikki,' added Gruber.

'They're not back yet, unfortunately,' said Matthews.

'Shall I go and see if I can round them up?' offered Benson.

'Vikki should be here any minute,' said Campbell.

Just then there was a bang on the door. Vikki was breathless with running. 'The students know something's up. I had to cut a lecture short this morning.'

'Never mind that,' said Gruber, completely unconscious of the havoc the students could cause if they cottoned on, especially if the psychic class managed to home in on these thoughts and ideas.

Vikki was edging up to Matthews but he had more important things to think about right now and moved over to the other side of the room near the Professor. 'After all,' he thought, 'I don't want to queer my pitch with Campbell and get left behind.'

The door opened again and Katie and Robert came in looking a bit scared. They had never been allowed to come into this inner sanctum before. 'Mark wanted to come, why couldn't he, Daddy?' said Katie querulously.

'There isn't room for any more people in here,' said Gruber. He and Benson were testing out the machine.

'We only want to test your voices,' added Benson.

'What's that, Daddy?' Katie ran over to the tape recorder.

'It's a tape recorder,' said Campbell.

'Now,' the Professor intervened, 'can we get on?' He strummed lightly at the harp. 'I obviously can't play the whole phrase I've worked out or I could find myself up there before you,' he said jovially. 'As soon as we begin to get near the right sounds the room will start vibrating. Come and stand by me, little girl.' He beckoned to Katie. 'I want you to sing these few notes.'

Katie tried to follow him as he played, singing as high as she could, but nothing happened. 'Not enough resonance,' said the Professor. Katie looked crestfallen.

Gruber looked at Vikki. 'Now you try.'

Vikki also trilled away but again there was no effect; just the rippling notes of the harp trailing away. After all, was it going to fail? Now it was Robert's turn and they all held their breath as Robert listened intently, took his place by the Professor, opened his mouth and brought forth some beautiful high notes.

The screen flickered violently and a loud trembling noise reverberated round the laboratory. Everyone was stunned. 'We must be nearly there,' said Gruber, thrilled with the outcome of the experiment. He turned the machine off. 'We'll have to be really careful or we could blow the machine,' Benson remarked.

84

'I agree, Benson. Now it's time for you to get your shape machine going.'

'Wait a minute,' interrupted the Professor, 'we must take great care. Once the last note is produced into the shape we will have to be in the spacecraft.'

Campbell and Matthews were annoyed that they could hardly follow this line of reasoning. 'What's this shape machine, then?' said Campbell grumpily.

'Bring us up to date,' added Matthews.

Gruber ignored them, immersed in thinking of the consequences of this discovery of Benson's.

'The Professor is right. If we are in here we will just hit the roof and be killed instantly.'

Robert, hearing this, piped up, 'Be blown to bits you mean?'

This remark also was ignored. No-one wanted to think of such a terrible thing happening.

Benson took Campbell and Matthews aside and briefly explained to them his new theory.

The Professor was now in his element. 'We should be able to get it all taped except the last note which young Robert will produce when we are all packed into the vehicle.'

'I still don't see how this is going to work,' said Campbell, looking puzzled.

'I think I can,' said Matthews. 'We'll have to wire the sound machine and the locater together into the electric circuit.'

'Of course, but it all sounds too simple.'

'And I presume it won't matter where we stand the equipment?' added Gruber.

'Right.'

'You're a clever chap, Matthews,' said Benson approvingly. 'After all, the answer to a complicated question is often very simple.'

'And as for young Robert here,' Campbell slapped him on the back, 'we won't be able to take off without him.'

Robert was quite overwhelmed. Katie was none too pleased. She would have liked to have been the king pin. Now she would have to put up with a lot of stick from Mark. Vikki was not sorry. She did not even know whether she wanted to be in on this hare-brained scheme.

'It seems to me the whole idea is like that Japanese hara-kiri thing,' she said rather disdainfully.

'You've no sense of adventure,' replied Campbell.

'You know you wouldn't like to be left behind,' said Matthews teasingly.

'Can we go now, Dad?' cried Katie, tossing back her long hair. Really, she'd had enough of all this. Now that it was obvious she was not going to be the centre of attention she was no longer interested in her father's work.

'Of course, dear, run along,' he said absent-mindedly.

'Coming, Robert?' she called.

Robert was busy looking at the screen and locater. He was fascinated. He did not even hear Katie calling him. She called again, crossly, 'Robert!'

'I want to look at this. Tell Mum I'll be back later.'

Katie flounced out of the room. Benson thought it a good idea that the boy should take an interest in the experiment and try to understand, especially as he now had such an important role. So he related to Robert what was happening and the meaning of the drawing on the locater.

'What does that shape remind you of?' he asked.

Robert peered at it intently. 'It looks like a tomato.'

'Well, well,' said Gruber overhearing that remark, 'who would have thought a tomato could be relative to the universe?'

'There are other fruits that shape you know,' said Benson.

'Green peppers?' suggested Campbell.

'Apples?' queried Matthews.

'They're not the same as a tomato,' insisted Robert. 'The pips are surrounded in a sort of liquid jelly.'

'Just like the brain,' observed Gruber.

'So in our universe the pips are the stars and galaxies,' enthused Benson.

'But what about the middle bit?' asked Matthews.

'Maybe the two sides implode after so many thousand million years into the middle and then explode again,' was Gruber's response.

'Then our universe is the middle bit, perhaps?' suggested Campbell.

'Also,' added Benson, 'when you think of it, the word

tomato is made up of the same letters as the word atom. Hmmm. . . perhaps there is something in Robert's idea.'

'I can see Robert will have to join our team,' said Campbell.

'Certainly it's something to think about when we have the time,' Benson was quite taken with this novel idea of a tomato.

Matthews then came up with his view. 'If the universe has a shape then there must be an edge to it.'

'All this philosophising isn't getting us to planet X,' interrupted Gruber. 'Enough talking, we must get back to work. You'd better get along home now, Robert and don't go far away. We shall be along to collect you all in next to no time.'

'A bit ambitious,' muttered Campbell.

Robert was disappointed that he could not stay longer, especially as they appeared interested in his remark about the tomato. Then the idea came to him. 'Why don't we call the planet "Toma"? That's atom and tomato as well.'

'Super,' Gruber spoke quickly. He did not want to be bothered now with thinking of names.

'Good lad,' said Benson approvingly. 'Wonderful idea – don't you think so?' He looked around and all nodded their agreement.

'That's it then, Toma it shall be.'

Robert went quietly home, thrilled to have made such an important decision as naming the new planet and with his head full of weird and wonderful shapes and sounds.

Vikki, who had not said a word, was not keen to stay. 'I'll try and find some coffee or tea and something to eat.'

They had all forgotten they were hungry and thirsty. The general concensus of opinion was that coffee or tea would be greatly appreciated. 'Be back soon,' she said and, with a sigh of relief, left the heavily charged atmosphere of the laboratory.

18

Vikki was hurrying round the back of the college to their flat to see what she could find in the way of food. Suddenly, a band of students barred her way. One detached himself from the crowd and spoke first, 'What's going on?'

'Nothing's going on,' replied Vikki, trying to get by him.

'Oh yes it it. We know, don't we?' He looked round at the rest of the crowd for assurance.

They replied in unison, 'Oh yes, we know.'

Vikki hedged backwards but Adam grabbed her by the arm. 'If you don't tell us then we'll have to strap you up to the clairaudient machine, won't we?' Again he looked at the crowd and again they cried, 'Yes, we will.'

'Stop playing about,' said Vikki angrily.

'Dear me,' Adam gave her a pull in the direction of the crowd. 'We're not playing games. We want to know.'

'We want to know,' chanted the crowd.

'Let me go.' Vikki was now becoming quite scared. There were so many of them and she was too far away from the lab to shout for help, not that they would have heard her anyway. Adam began to pull her along and another student, a tall girl with big teeth, black fuzzy hair and dark skin, grabbed hold of her other arm. They dragged her to the college doors and pushed and pulled her inside, down the corridor and into the room where they did psychic experiments. Vikki was horrified. She felt trapped like an animal waiting to be slaughtered. Only this would be mental butchery, not physical. 'How,' she thought as they strapped her into a chair which looked very similar to a dentist's chair, 'am I going to stop myself from telling what I know?'

Adam had already read her thoughts. 'You won't be able to stop yourself from telling us, because this machine is clairaudient. Every thought you have will be spoken out loud.'

Vikki looked at the sea of faces surveying her with different expressions – militant, angry, grim. Then, as Adam touched the 'on' button the expressions turned to one of expectancy and after a few seconds they became blurred and all dissolved into one another until they became just one big face.

'You can let her go now, Meryl,' said Adam. Meryl relaxed her grip. 'It will only take a few minutes,' he continued. 'Soon she'll be tuned in and then we can ask the questions.' There was a general hubbub of murmuring and remarks from the rest. 'Be quiet,' hissed Adam, 'or we might miss something.'

A light came on in the middle of the ingenious looking contraption which rested like a crown on her head. Her mouth opened as if to speak but no sound came forth. 'She's trying to resist,' said Meryl.

'I'll have to give her a shot then.' Adam went to a cupboard and took a bottle and syringe. He carefully filled the syringe and came over to Vikki.

'Roll up her sleeve,' he said to Meryl, who obediently obliged. Adam plunged the syringe into Vikki's arm.

The room was deathly quiet as they waited for the shot to take effect. Suddenly Vikki sat bolt upright and startled them to death. This was most unusual. It was as if a corpse had moved by itself. All the senses that activated the muscles were supposed to be completely sedated by now. Most of the students were now beginning to feel decidedly jittery. They gasped when her voice boomed out, 'The tomato will not speak.'

There wasn't a sound until Adam spoke. 'What the Hell does that mean?'

'Has something gone wrong with the machine?' said Meryl, just as perplexed.

There was a general murmuring from the crowd, now subdued, knowing that something was going on which they could not understand. They were intrigued. No-one had ever been able to go above the memory searcher. And what was 'the tomato'?

'Perhaps you've given her too much sedative,' said one lad.

'Surely that would make the brain less active,' said another.

'A remark like that must come from the superconscious,' voiced a young Indian girl.

'You mean outside the brain?' asked another girl.

'Of course. Isn't that what clairaudience is all about? You shouldn't be in the psychic class if you can't even comprehend that,' said Adam impatiently.

Vikki was lying back in the chair now, stiff as a board. 'She should be relaxed now, not like this,' Adam shouted to the crowd. 'Does anyone have any ideas why this happened?'

'Perhaps she's been activated by something else,' ventured one.

'Aha,' Adam suddenly perked up, 'she's just come from the lab hasn't she? They must be a lot further ahead than we realise.'

Gradually the murmurings became louder, the students began to voice their thoughts vociferously.

'Why should we be left out?'

'Give her another shot.'

'I don't think that will do any good,' said Adam thoughtfully. 'We'll just have to leave her until it wears off.'

'What shall we do now?' asked Meryl desperately.

'Let's go over to the lab,' was one opinion which was soon taken up by all.

'Good idea,' agreed Adam. 'That's what we'll do.'

They all cheered. Feelings ran high. If there was a riot, so what? It only needed one person to say, 'Charge!'

'I think you lot should stay here,' said Adam, 'while Meryl and I see if we can find out what's happening.'

There was an angry roar. This was not good enough. The same thought ran through them all. 'Those two might get themselves included in whatever is going on and we will be left behind like so much dross.'

'Come on,' said one tall, gangly youth and they swept as one towards the door and surged down the corridor like a swarm of bees.

19

Mary and Nora were both engrossed in their own thoughts, having run out of conversation – each terrified of their children being used in an experiment beyond their comprehension. Mary breathed a sigh of relief as she heard Katie run up the path. She jumped out of her chair and went to open the door. Katie came in looking like a thundercloud.

'What's the matter, dear?' Mary said, only too glad to have her home.

Mark was watching a film on video but looked up as she came in. Katie slumped into a chair and did not reply.

'Come on then,' teased Mark. 'Weren't you any good?'

'What did they want you for?' asked Nora, 'and where's Robert?'

'They're going to use his voice,' said Katie grumpily.

'What for?' repeated Nora. This didn't sound too bad. She'd had visions of Robert being strapped into some computerised contraption.

'Voice?' said Mary perplexed. 'What voice?'

'For the sound waves,' said Katie, exasperated.

'Oh,' said Mary weakly and sat down again. This was all too much. What nonsense – sound waves and voices. Was there no stopping this husband of hers?

'It sounds grotesque,' broke in Mark. 'What did you have to do?' He spoke in a more conciliatory tone. After all, he wanted to know and if he kept teasing her she wouldn't say a word.

Now that she was the centre of attention Katie thought she might just tell them what was going on in the lab. 'Well,' she said slowly, savouring every moment, knowing they were all agog, 'this is what happened. The Professor was playing the harp and I had to sing some notes. Then Vikki had to sing and then. . .' she paused for breath, 'Robert had to sing and there was this tremendous noise and the whole room was pounding with noise. It was really quite frightening.' She stopped to see what effect this was having on her audience. They just gaped. Nobody could think of anything to say.

'Is Robert still there?' Nora managed to ask.

'Of course,' said Katie simply. 'He'll be back soon. They can't do any more with him in case the lab goes up into space.' She waited to see what effect this had.

'Now you're just making things up,' said Mary crossly.

'No I'm not,' shouted Katie.

'Fancy, my Robert,' Nora wept. 'Oh, if only Don were here.'

'Now, don't take on so. Don will come back soon, you'll see,' said Mary putting an arm round her to console her.

'What about those two men?' Mark cried. He suddenly remembered they were supposed to come back home with them.

'What two men?' asked Mary.

'You know, the one who dropped on the doorstep and the one in the plane.'

'Oooh,' said Katie. 'We had a race here. We forgot all about them.'

'Shall I go and look for them?' enquired Mark as he got up and went to the door.

'No you don't,' shouted Mary. 'You stay here, it's nearly dark. Let them find their own way.'

Just then Robert arrived looking very pleased with himself. They looked at him as if he were from another world. He went and sat near Mark.

'Pity you couldn't have come over, it was really great.'

Then they all bombarded him with questions.

'What are they doing over there?'

'Where are they taking you?'

'What's this about your voice?'

'Don't all talk at once,' said Robert in a superior tone.

'Your Dad,' he looked at Mark, 'is a genius. He's found a way to travel to another planet through sound waves.'

'What nonsense,' cried Mary.

Nora didn't know whether to agree with Robert or Mary. 'Are we all going, then?' she asked.

'I want to go, I want to go,' repeated Katie, bouncing up and down on a chair.

'I don't know,' said Robert, 'I suppose so. You should have seen the picture of the galaxy. It was awesome.'

'You mean Dad's found a planet in another galaxy for us?' said Mark unbelievingly.

'That's right. And there were all these funny shapes they kept talking about as well.'

'What sort of shapes?' enquired Nora.

'Oh, fruit and stuff like that.'

'Fruit?'

'And people's insides, and brains.'

'It's beginning to sound a bit horrific.'

'Like one of those horror movies,' Katie interrupted.

'But where does your voice come in?' asked Nora.

'I'm not sure − I couldn't sing it else the whole place might have blown.'

'The whole room shook, Mummy,' said Katie knowingly.

'I thought of the name for it,' Robert swelled up with pride.

'What name?' pouted Katie. She had left the laboratory before this had been mentioned.

'Toma!'

'That's a silly name.'

'I think I've heard enough.' Mary got up to go into the kitchen.

'I expect they'll come for us soon.' Robert had absolute confidence in Dr Gruber.

'Sounds like a death knell to me,' replied Mary. 'I'm not listening to any more. I've heard enough for one day.'

'Just think,' Mark said dreamily, 'tomorrow we could be living in a new world!'

How many people had said that before.

20

Much to his amazement Don managed to land safely, apart from a few bruises, on a small patch of ground, just mising some large trees by the side of a road. 'Thank God,' he said to himself, 'I'm still in one piece. It's a miracle I didn't break my legs. I wonder how far I am from Berry Hill?'

He unharnessed the parachute, feeling weak at the knees, but the thought of getting back home gave him a spurt of energy and he started walking in what he hoped was the right direction. After a short while of trudging along the road he came upon a large house that he recognised. He now felt he had wings on his feet and soon he came to the road leading to Berry Hill from the opposite side to his own home. His heart thumped with eager anticipation.

'What a Godamned idiot I've been,' he thought as he broke into a jog. Then, out of the mist in the distance he could see the plane. 'That wasn't there when I left. Something must have happened.' He tried to run faster and at last he saw the familiar house where they had lived for so many years.

'What's that noise?' He could hear the shouts and cries of the students as they went rampaging towards Gruber's laboratory. Then he saw them. They seemed to be coming from all directions, swarming across the college grounds, running down the road from the front gate and across the field at the back, gaining more and more students as they went. 'I don't want to get mixed up in that lot. I'll try and get round the back way.'

He made for the lane which ran along the back of his and Gruber's house, but just as he was approaching it a herd of students came yelling down the lane, almost crushing him against the wall. He managed to pull himself over a part of the wall that was broken and ran into the back of the college. By this time most of the students had disappeared towards the lab. News that Gruber was way ahead of them in some experiment had come through from the Class of Psychic Studies and was spreading like wildfire. Panic, fear and anger were rampant.

Don was absolutely exhausted and opened a door, hoping to find a room where he could flop down into a chair. He looked round furtively and to his consternation saw Vikki strapped to a chair with some weird contraption on her head. She was just beginning to come round and her eyes beseeched him to do something quickly. He went over to her and tried to figure out how to extract her from the queer appliance. Vikki managed to raise her hand weakly and point to the wall.

'Do I touch that?' he asked, pointing to a red spot on the wall.

Vikki flapped her hand in acquiescence. He put his finger to the red spot which immediately turned off the power and he found he was able to remove the contraption from her head. 'Thank God you've come,' she said hoarsely.

'What have they done to you?'

'They were trying to get information out of me about Dr Gruber's work,' she said. 'I remember them asking me questions but I can't remember if I told them anything or not. They gave me an injection and I passed out.'

'They all seemed to be charging in the direction of the lab. Do you think. . .'

Vikki interrupted. 'Oh no,' she was wide awake now, 'Jim and the others, they've found the secret.' It all came back to her now. She was going to her apartment to see if there was any coffee left in her cupboard which she kept locked up. Only she never reached the flat.

'We must get to the lab quickly,' she cried fearfully. 'They'll all be massacred!'

'But how can we? We won't be able to fight our way through that lot.'

'Your Robert was in the lab with them,' said Vikki,

knowing this would get him going. 'It's his voice they're going to use.'

'Robert!' Don's face went white. 'And Nora, is she there as well?'

'No, I think she's at home.'

'We've got to get through to the lab somehow and warn them. Is there a phone here?' He looked round wildly.

'Only in the corridor.'

'Right. Let's start with that,' said Don in a dictatorial tone. Had he not led the tribe through the forest of dinosaurs? Although God knows what had happened to them. Was he going to let a few students frighten him? Not likely! 'Gird your loins, man, and tackle this problem.' The dinosaurs – he had completely forgotten about them. How far had they progressed? If they were stampeding in this direction. . .

Vikki broke in on his thoughts. 'Come on then, let's phone.'

'Have you got the extension number?'

Vikki panicked. 'I can't remember it!'

'There must be a list somewhere.'

'Yes, but not in here,' replied Vikki. 'This isn't a lecture room. It's for psychic experiments.'

'Well then, can't we use one of these machines to get the number?' Don looked around the room at the various machines.

'I wanted to learn more about this psychic work but my lectures always clashed. There's a simple one here.' Vikki went over to a small keyboard attached to several wires which were plugged into the floor. There was a small audio cassette player with headphones attached and a lead connecting itto the keyboard.

'What do you have to do?' asked Don. He had never seen a machine which was supposed to give psychic messages.

'You type out your question on this keyboard and the answer is supposed to come through the headphones.'

Vikki sat down and put the headphones on, pressed the 'on' key and then typed out her question – 'What is the telephone number of the college laboratory?'

She waited expectantly. Don impatiently tapped his foot. 'Don't do that – it has to be absolute quiet.'

Slightly muffled, but nevertheless clear enough to be

understood, came the answer, 'Number does not exist.'

'There's no such number.'

They looked at each other, aware of impending disaster.

'Of course,' Vikki suddenly remembered, 'there isn't a phone in the lab in case it interrupts some vital experiment.'

'But there must be a phone nearby,' said Don in desperation.

'In the room next door, probably. But they wouldn't hear it anyway.'

'Oh my God, I've got to get Robert out of there.'

Don shot out of the door and ran down the corridor, hardly knowing where he was going in his fever of anxiety.

'Wait for me. . .' Vikki ran after him, not wanting to be left alone in that room.

21

Benson and Gruber were now satisfied that they had all the notes of the Professor's music on tape; all the rippling notes of the harp and Robert's voice blending in at the appropriate moment except for the last high note which, hopefully, would result in take-off. Benson had tested out his shape machine on the locater, liaising with the Professor to make sure there was perfect balance between the notes and the shape.

'We have to make sure one side of the "tomato" isn't bigger than the other,' said Benson.

'It certainly seems a bit hit or miss,' said Gruber, 'but we've no time for perfection.'

'We'll have to pray to the Gods,' Matthews chimed in. He was busy working out equations on the blackboard.

'If it goes wrong we may find ourselves with the Gods,' replied Benson.

'We must be positive,' said Gruber.

Campbell found he could not concentrate. 'Why has Vikki not returned?' He had a very odd feeling that something had happened to her. 'Vikki should be back by now,' he said uneasily.

'Oh, you know what women are,' replied Matthews airily. 'She's probably nattering to someone en route.'

'I've got a nasty feeling. . .' Campbell broke off to listen.

Benson turned round. 'You can't hear anything in here, old chap, it's sound-proofed.'

'I know, I know. . . I think I'll go and see where she's got to,' said Campbell, walking to the door. He had hardly been gone a second when he was back in again looking really startled. 'Phew!' he exclaimed.

'What's the matter, man? Your hair's standing on end,' remarked Matthews.

Gruber and Benson looked annoyed. They didn't want anyone or anything to upset their wonderful plan. The slightest hitch was a matter of life and death.

'I must have had a premonition,' Campbell burst out. 'It's the students. . . they're coming over here in droves!'

'Christ!' exploded Benson, for once his normal aplomb leaving him. 'Bolt the door!'

The Professor seemed to shrivel and Gruber became wild-eyed with anger. Campbell bolted the door with shaking hands. 'What now?' he said. 'They'll only break it down.'

'They could get through the window in the next room if they come round the back,' added Benson.

Matthews looked up at the ceiling. 'Praise the Lord, what's that?' he pointed to a rectangular piece of wood with a small hook on it in the middle of the ceiling.

'It was a skylight,' said Gruber. 'We had it boarded over because of the daylight getting in.'

'D'you think we could get out that way?' said Campbell hopefully.

'I won't be able to get the harp through there,' twittered the Professor.

'That's all right, Professor,' said Benson soothingly. 'You won't need the harp any more – we've got it all on tape.'

'Oh yes, of course, of course,' nodded the Professor.

'Come on then,' Campbell was eager to have a go. 'Matthews, help me move this table.'

Together they moved a lot of paraphernalia off the table and lifted it up and placed it underneath the skylight. 'You're the tallest, Matthews, see if you can open it,' said Campbell.

Matthews pushed and pulled but could not shift it. 'Don't hang about, man, break the bloody glass,' shouted Gruber, seething with impatience.

'Hand me up a chair then.'

Gruber lifted up a small swivel chair. Matthews grabbed it and smashed it against the painted glass.

'What about the equipment?' shouted Benson.

'The students,' Campbell went white. 'They'll hear it.'

'I should think they're making too much noise themselves,' said Matthews, poking his head out of the skylight.

Gruber dashed over to the remote control and switched everything off. There was a deathly silence. Then they could hear the cries and shouts of the angry mob. 'You go first, Gruber,' said Benson, 'and I'll hand you the tape recorder and machine.'

Campbell picked up a small case which had been pushed under the table. 'Hey, this is a Godsend,' and quickly he opened it and packed in the tape recorder and Benson's shape machine, zipped it up and handed it to Matthews who managed to get out of the window onto the flat roof. Gruber heaved himself up and joined Matthews and Benson.

Matthews handed the case to Gruber and shouted down, 'What about the Professor?'

'Don't worry about me. I've done my work. I'm too old for this sort of thing. I'll only be a hindrance to you,' he said with a sigh.

'Nonsense,' Gruber now spoke to him. 'We may need you. Help him up, Campbell.'

Campbell lifted the Professor onto the table and Matthews grabbed hold of his wrists and lifted him through the skylight. Campbell followed. From the rooftop they could see the students swarming round. Fortunately, none of them bothered to look up. They were more intent on getting into the laboratory.

'How are we going to get down?' hissed Gruber.

'This way,' Campbell beckoned as they crept along the flat roof until they came to another skylight.

'Oh, not again,' quavered the Professor.

'I don't know where this leads to, but here goes,' and Matthews yanked open the window and peered down. Underneath he could see a flat topped electric cooker. Next to it was a double drainer sink and the whole room was completely enclosed with built-in cupboards. There was an old table in the middle of the room.

'Look,' whispered Campbell to Gruber, 'there's no way out.' He made way for Gruber to have a look.

Gruber pursed his lips. 'There's always a way out,' he said

grimly. This was his favourite maxim. 'Get going.' He almost pushed Campbell through the skylight. With a shrug Campbell lowered himself down and landed safely on the cooker, followed by Gruber.

'You go next,' said Matthews to Benson, 'and I'll hand down the Professor.' He spoke as if the Professor were a small parcel. Benson agreed and dropped onto the top of the cooker.

'Frying tonight,' chuckled Matthews.

'Shut up,' hissed Benson.

'I don't want to go down there,' whined the Professor.

'Oh yes you do,' said Matthews as he picked up the Professor and pushed him down through the window.

'Ohhh. . .' the Professor groaned as he hung by his wrists for the second time.

'Give me a hand,' said Benson to Campbell. Campbell got back onto the cooker and managed to catch the Professor as he swung towards him like a monkey and in turn lowered him down to Benson. Eventually they were all safely on the ground.

Gruber had been going round opening the cupboard doors. 'Look at this, they're full of food.' Every cupboard was stacked with all manner of tinned and dried foods.

'Whatever is this? Looks like an old fashioned barrel of beer,' exclaimed Campbell.

'Trust you to find that,' said Matthews.

Benson and Gruber went over to look. Sure enough, there was a wooden barrel with a tap on it. Gruber inspected it and turned on the tap. Out came a spurt of water. 'Well I'm damned,' said Campbell, 'it must be a well.'

'What's the meaning of all this?' queried Matthews. 'Were they expecting a siege?'

'It must be the room where they kept all the food in case of nuclear attack,' replied Benson.

'So the nuclear shelter must be nearby,' mused Gruber. He went on investigating the cupboards until he came to one which was completely empty.

'It would have to be miles underground, surely?' said Campbell.

Gruber was running his fingers round the inside of the empty cupboard. He crouched on the floor. 'This is it,' he cried and suddenly the floor of the cupboard sprang up like a jack-in-the-box nearly hitting him on the chin, revealing steps going down into the bowels of the earth.

'Jesus,' exclaimed Matthews.

'Just a minute,' said Benson as Gruber started climbing down the stairs, 'we don't know if it leads anywhere.'

'That's a point,' said Campbell, 'this might be the only entrance.'

'You pessimists. We'll have to find out, won't we. . .' Gruber's voice trailed away as he disappeared down the steps. 'You won't get far in the dark,' shouted Benson after him.

'Let's find the light,' Matthews looked into the cupboard but could see no indication of a light switch.

'The switch must be hidden,' said Campbell, 'we'll have to run our fingers over every bit of the wall.'

'It's more likely to be under the floor,' said Benson.

'Aha, you're right as usual Benson,' said Campbell as he found the concealed switch on the wall by the first step.

'Let there be light,' quoted Matthews.

'Why don't we take some of this food with us?' said Campbell collecting a few tins and packets together. 'In fact, why don't we have a snack now to keep us going?'

'Good idea,' replied Benson, 'but there's no holding Gruber now he can see where he's going.'

'Here are some packs of dinner pills. They'll be useful and don't take up much room. Is there a bag anywhere?'

Benson found a refuse sack and helped Campbell throw the food into it. Matthews joined in. 'Cans of drink here, any beer I wonder?'

'We can't stop to eat now,' said Benson, 'better take as much as we can.'

'One pill will keep us going for a day,' added Campbell. Benson tied a knot in the sack and down the steps they went in pursuit of Gruber who had disappeared from view.

22

Don and Vikki looked at each other, wondering what to do next. 'What now?' asked Vikki apprehensively. They stood in the main doorway of the college and heard the noise of the students pounding round to the laboratory. Some were trying to climb up drainpipes and it seemed to be general pandemonium.

'We can only hope they've managed to get out of the lab.'

'I know where they'll make for.'

'Where's that?' said Don.

'The plane that landed on top of Berry Hill,' replied Vikki.

'I saw that when I came down in my parachute.'

'Parachute?'

'There's no time to tell you about that now,' said Don hurriedly. 'I think you may be right. Let's find the plane. Where are they thinking of going, then? North Africa?'

'Vikki laughed. 'Heavens no – it's planet Toma they're aiming for.'

'You're joking,' exclaimed Don.

'No I'm not. You wouldn't believe what I heard in that laboratory.'

'I took old Gruber for a bit of a madman,' mused Don.

'He may be for all I know,' said Vikki, 'but he got that Professor of Music over and they've come up with this weird idea of using voice and harp strings.' She paused.

'Go on.'

'And I saw these stars on the screen and Dr Gruber said where the light was bleeping was this planet they've found which is called Toma.'

'But I still don't see. . .'

'Well, evidently it was the sound coming from it which was so important.'

'Oh I see, you mean they were trying to produce the same sound on a musical instrument?'

'That's it, and that is where Robert's voice came into it as well.'

'Well I'm damned.' Don was overawed to think that his son could be of such importance. 'Perhaps old Gruber is a genuis after all.'

'Could be, but I think we should make tracks for that plane, not stand around here.'

'You're right, agreed Don. 'Is there another way out?'

Vikki led the way out to the back of the college. The yelling seemed to have died down. They saw a few students hanging around outside the laboratory building but they managed to run in the opposite direction across what used to be a tennis court and scramble through a hole in the fence. 'Phew,' said Don breathlessly, 'that was close.'

Vikki led the way down the lane which opened out onto the road. 'We'll just have to run for it,' she whispered.

They dashed across the road and made for Berry Hill and the sanctuary of the trees and bushes. In any event, it was now dark and they could not be easily seen. Don looked back. 'I can see people on the roof of the laboratory,' he said.

'That's it,' exclaimed Vikki. 'They must have escaped through the roof somehow.'

'Good God, in that case they've either got to the plane by now or they've gone a different way.'

'It seems hopeful,' puffed Vikki as they clambered on, not looking back, fearful of being pursued. They stopped for a moment, exhausted with their exertions, and sat on an old tree stump to get their breath. There was no sound except for a few screams in the distance. After a few minutes Don got up, anxious to find his son.

'Come on,' he pleaded, taking her arm and helping her up. Just as he did so, there was a rustling noise which sent a prickle down their spines. 'Expect it's rats,' he whispered. 'We're plagued with them now.'

'Of course, it's only rats,' said Vikki, relieved.

'She had visions of students pouncing on them thinking

they would lead them to the scientists. Then the rustling noise became louder until it was the noise of a stampede, like a herd of elephants crashing through the bushes. Vikki clutched at Don in terror and they stood frozen to the spot as they saw two dinosaurs with two little ones following, heading full pelt down the hill. 'Are we in a nightmare?' asked Vikki in a whisper. 'There's no such thing as dinosaurs. They've been extinct for millions of years. We must be hallucinating.'

'No we're not,' replied Don. 'I've been through this before. I didn't have time to tell you about it.' Shaking with fear, Vikki grabbed Don's arm.

'Come on,' said Don, once again the commander.

On the way up the hill he told Vikki of his trek through the forest, about the old sea captain and the poor souls who must now be perishing on their way across the Channel, about the young couple and Hercules and how Hercules had let him have the balloon to get back.

Vikki was enthralled listening to his story and so on they went picking their way over the stones, the night air becoming more murky with the stench of rotting vegetation and the indigo mist swirling around the threadbare branches of the trees and bushes.

Don stopped and listened. 'I can hear something else.'

'So can I,' said Vikki uneasily. 'I think it's voices.'

'Friend or foe, I wonder.'

'At least it's human.'

Through the mist they could see the two men coming towards them. There was no going back so eventually they met face to face. Don recognised Philip with relief. 'God, you startled us.'

'And we thought you were dinosaurs,' said Philip. 'By the way, this is my friend Ben.'

'And this is Vikki, Campbell's wife,' added Don.

Once introductions had been exchanged, they agreed to join forces. So they continued trekking up the hill.

'I want to know what's going on,' said Ben in exasperation.

'I'm pretty much in the dark myself,' added Don.

'I'll try and explain what I heard in the laboratory as we go along,' said Vikki.

She did her best with the scant information she had gleaned while the scientists were experimenting with their sounds and voices. 'And,' she finished, 'the ludicrous finale to all this is going to be in the plane.'

'I just can't believe it,' said Ben shaking his head in disbelief.

'Well, we must plough on. I saw it when I was coming down in the parachute so it must be near.'

'You sound as if you've had a few adventures too,' said Ben admiringly.

'Yes,' Don sighed, 'I think I've been through more in the last two days than I have in the whole of my life.'

'We got lost on the way back to Gruber's house – saw a dinosaur, you know,' said Ben, thinking they would not believe him.

'So did we,' said Don and Vikki together.

'Oh yes, it's quite true,' added Don. 'I saw two people and a child trampled to death by them.'

Vikki shivered. 'It's a nightmare. How can it be real?'

Philip did not join in to reminisce about his own experience. He did not want to remind Ben of how he had left him to die, so he trudged on ahead.

'There it is,' he called excitedly.

Yes, there was the plane only a short distance away from them. Nearly on their knees they scrambled up the hill, mindless of the thicket scratching at them and tearing their clothes, only one thought in their minds, 'escape!'

23

Benson, Campbell, Matthews and the Professor were wending their way through the nuclear shelter – past line after line of bunk beds, lounging areas and showers, through a library full of books and a television and computer room. 'Gruber,' shouted Benson, 'where the Devil's he got to?'

'They've got it all here, haven't they?' said Campbell.

'Under our very noses and we didn't even know it existed,' replied Benson.

'Where do you think it comes out?' enquired Campbell.

'Come on Matthews, you should be able to figure it out.'

'Probably near the railway station,' was his reply.'

'I can't keep up with you young things,' gasped the Professor.

'Sorry old man,' said Matthews. 'We'll slow down.'

'Where's Gruber?' Benson said, getting agitated. After all, Gruber had the new invention with him. Campbell also realised something was amiss. There was no sight or sound of Gruber down the corridor.

'D'you think he's found another way out?' volunteered the Professor. 'You know what a madcap he is.' They all looked at each other.

'Well, if he has found another way, he'll go straight home to get his family and Robert,' said Benson reassuringly.

'Yes,' agreed Campbell, 'the best thing we can do is just plough on and get to the plane. He'll know that.'

'Do you know, Benson,' said Campbell, 'we haven't even thought of who we are going to take with us?'

'That's right, Gruber is the only one with a family.'

Campbell was worried about Vikki. 'I wonder if Vikki will

be able to get to the plane?' he murmured.

Matthews was looking after the Professor. He heard Campbell's remark but it only made him realise that he did not care very much whether he saw Vikki again or not.

'How many people do you think we could get into the plane?' asked Benson.

'Well it's supposed to seat eight,' replied Matthews, 'but I should think we might squeeze twelve in.'

'Perhaps a few more at a push,' added Campbell.

'If they were pygmies,' said Matthews.

'Don't forget three of them will be children,' Benson added.

'We really need a few youngsters,' said Campbell, 'but we've had to keep the whole thing so secret, how could we just pick out one or two?'

'I suppose we ought to take a few young people with us if we're going to colonise a new planet,' said Benson.

'Unless it's already inhabited,' chipped in Matthews.

'Good God.' Benson was alarmed at this prospect. 'That never occurred to me.'

'Something to think about, isn't it Professor?' Matthews was helping him along. The Professor shook his head.

'Perhaps we could be like the Mormons,' chuckled Matthews, 'half a dozen wives each.'

'Don't be an idiot,' said Benson, 'we shall only have two or three women with us.'

'Unless we round up a few female students,' Matthews said with relish.

'Vikki wouldn't stand for it, that's a cert,' said Campbell.

'Somehow I've got to find her,' he thought to himself.

Benson had gone on ahead and shouted back, 'There's some steps up here.'

The others put a spurt on and caught up with him, the Professor puffing and panting. They could see the steps going up and up to where. . . ?

'I'd better investigate,' said Benson and he started up. A minute later he shouted, 'Come and help with this.'

Campbell leapt up the steps and saw Benson trying to open a manhole cover in the ceiling.

'Here, let me have a go,' said Campbell, and with a swift turn of the metal handle he gingerly opened the cover and looked out. All was quiet so he lifted himself out. The others followed. Sure enough they were close to the railway line but quite a long way from the station.

'Should we go back to Gruber's to see if he's there?' asked Benson.

'I think we should try and find the plane,' replied Campbell and Matthews together.

'I could go back for Gruber,' piped up the Professor. He knew they could manage quite well without him now so it didn't really matter whether he went with them or not. They all demurred at this but then agreed that perhaps it was a sensible idea. The Professor would be able to tell Gruber that they were heading straight for the plane.

'Sure you'll be O.K?' Matthews asked sympathetically.

'Yes, yes, thank you. I'll see you anon,' and off he went. He really felt he'd had enough excitement for one day.

24

Adam and Meryl pounded on the laboratory door although the red light was on showing 'no admittance'.

'Perhaps they're in the middle of an experiment,' said Meryl.

'I don't care what they're doing,' replied Adam. 'Whatever it is, I'm going to find out,' and he continued banging and pushing against the door. More and more students were pounding behind them.

'Give me a hand,' cried Adam, 'we'll have to break it down.'

None of them looked very strong, with a lack of proper food, but two or three came forward shouting, 'Get the buggers out. . . no bloody door's going to stop me.'

So Adam and two others hurled themselves at the door and there was a gradual creaking.

'Once more might do it,' said Adam catching his breath.

Again they rammed the door and this time the door splintered and the crowd surged forward falling over the broken door. Meryl, although a pretty tough girl, could not get through quick enough. She screamed as she fell and others just trampled on her. Adam looked round but could not reach her. Hands and arms seemed to be flying everywhere.

It was not long before the whole laboratory was in ruins. All the fear, aggression and anger of the students at being left out of this potential escape route turned into a rampage of destruction.

Adam was clever enough to realise that this sort of behaviour would not help them in their predicament. He noticed some of the students who had fallen had blood on

110

their hands and faces from the broken glass which had fallen from the skylight. He looked up and saw where the scientists had made their exit.

'They're on the roof,' he shouted. 'After them,' and he picked up the table which had been overturned in the maelstrom, jumped onto it and heaved himself through the skylight.

'Adam,' cried Meryl, who was battered and bruised but still conscious. Was the bastard going to leave her behind? Adam did not hear her cries. He was like a bloodhound on the scent of a villain. He stood on the roof and saw those students who had got out of the crush and were milling about the grounds.

One young girl cried out, 'There's another skylight open over there,' and pointed to the other end of the building. 'You're right,' and he ran across the roof to the next skylight. 'I know what this is,' he thought, 'it's the opening to the nuclear shelter that's never been used.' And he gave a snort of satisfaction. 'Come on chaps,' he shouted to those behind him. And so they disappeared down into the shelter. They followed Adam as if he were the Pied Piper of Hamelin.

Meryl dragged herself up from the floor. Most of the others had fled. There were some like herself who had been pushed and trodden on, some still bleeding from the cuts they had received from falling onto the broken glass. They looked around and one said, 'Isn't there a first aid box anywhere?'

They all trooped out of the laboratory as best they could with their injuries and headed back towards the college. It was then that they heard a terrible roaring and threshing noise and suddenly, like an avalanche, a herd of dinosaurs came stampeding towards them. The students screamed and ran in all directions to try and get out of the way. Meryl crept towards the old tennis court and quite unwittingly followed in the footsteps of Don and Vikki. Although still in a state of shock, she managed to get a good way towards Berry Hill. She looked back and saw, to her horror, a blaze of light. Sparks were sizzling in all directions like a giant firework show and she could see two dinosaurs had got caught up in the great dish and had been instantly

111

electrocuted.

In the flow of light she could see students being trampled on by the dinosaurs in their frenzy to get away from the dish. The poor beasts were roaring in their agony and the students were screaming in terror, trying to hide from the holocaust. Meryl's one instinct was to get as far away as possible from the terrifying scene of carnage.

Meanwhile, Adam and those who had followed him, went the same way as the scientists until they took a different corridor and found themselves climbing up some winding stairs which led to a square manhole. Some had lagged behind, looking with wonder at the facilities which had been prepared underground.

'Hey, let's have a shower,' said one.

'I think I'll just have a kip.' One young girl stretched out on one of the comfortable bunk beds.

'You'll get left behind,' said her boyfriend.

'Come and lie down with me then,' she cajoled. 'Where are we going anyway?'

'Why don't we just stay here and partake of the goodies?' others asked.

Adam, still in the lead, jerked open the manhole, clambered out and found himself at the end of the platform at Perryn Halt. 'That shelter must have several exits,' he said. 'This one doesn't seem to lead us anywhere.'

'Here, what's this?' called out a young ginger-haired girl as she picked up a box of meal pills.

Adam grabbed the box from her and spoke knowingly. 'I bet those toe-rags took these from the shelter.'

'That means we're on the same path.'

'But which way have they gone?' asked another.

'How about up the hill?'

So it was agreed and up the hill they crawled like ants swarming over an ant heap.

'I reckon this is a long way round to the top of Berry Hill,' Adam reflected.

'But at least we've got out of the way of the dinosaurs,' said the ginger-haired girl.

And so up and up they went, discoursing amongst themselves the probabilities of what the scientists were up to. Then, in a sudden clearing, even though it was dark,

112

Adam let out a roar, 'Meryl!' He could just see her clawing her way through the dead bracken.

Meryl looked round and went on, taking no notice of him. Why should she? Had she not been left behind? This incensed Adam and he shouted again, 'Wait!'

But Meryl did not wait, she kept going. 'If there is any way out of this place I'm going and he can go to Hell,' she thought angrily. Then her hopes rose – what was that only a short distance away? She could see the outline of the plane and a figure standing by it waving to her. Her heart thumped with excitement and exertion – was it something good or bad? She did not bother to think any more, she just ran towards him, with Adam and his followers in hot pursuit.

25

Dr Gruber realised he had not given much thought to his family. In fact, from the scientific point of view, of course, Robert was the most important. Without him they would not be going anywhere. He hoped Nora wouldn't try and stop him. Almost unaware that he had left the others behind he went down one corridor after another, eventually arriving at a door. Frantically he unlocked it and started walking up the stone steps which wound round and round until he could see the dim outline of shrubs and trees.

'Where the devil am I?' he thought in consternation, not knowing that he had inadvertently given the students the slip. He walked up a long disused path and soon came to the very road which led to his house. He breathed a sigh of relief. He ran towards his house, still clutching the case and forgetting the others he had left behind. He could hear the noise of shouting and general pandemonium in the distance. He went round the back of the house and burst through the back door.

'Hurry up, we've got to go now,' he shouted.

Mary came into the kitchen and gasped when she saw her husband dirty and dishevelled and out of breath with running. 'Here, sit down. What on earth have you been doing? I'll get some hot water for you to have a wash. You'll feel better when you've changed your clothes,' she said soothingly.

'There's no time,' said Gruber. 'Where are the children?'

'What on earth do you mean?' said Mary, thoroughly bewildered.

Nora and the children joined them in the kitchen to see what was going on. 'Calm down, dear,' said Mary. 'We've

114

just been watching the screen. The flooding has stopped. Everything is going to be all right.'

'Everything is not going to be all right,' said Gruber, exasperated beyond endurance. 'You are all coming with me.'

'We're not going anywhere,' said Mary stubbornly. 'The whole thing is ridiculous. I don't suppose you'll even get off the ground.'

Gruber turned to Nora with a helpless shrug of his shoulders. 'Can't you make her see. . . ?' and then turned to Katie, Mark and Robert. 'Come along, there's no time to lose,' and started towards the door.

Nora did not really care whether she went or not. She certainly didn't want the responsibility of making anyone else's mind up for them. As Robert seemed important to this mission then she would, of course, go along too, but who was to know the outcome of such a venture? Perhaps Mary was right, it was just a stupid dream.

'You've got to come,' entreated Robert looking round at them all.

'No,' cried Mary. 'You're not taking them on your silly old machine,' and she grabbed hold of Mark and Katie.

Mark broke away. 'But I want to go,' he said despairingly.

'No, no,' cried Mary, beginning to get frightened now. What had seemed to be just another of her husband's silly notions was now taking a serious turn.

'Hurry up,' said Gruber, 'we can't hang about any longer. We've set the sound to blast off at ten o'clock and it's gone nine now.'

'We can't leave Mum on her own,' faltered Mark, torn between his Mother and Father.

'I forbid you to stay behind,' said Gruber fiercely. He wasn't used to having to use authority with the children. He had always left decisions regarding them to Mary so that now it was a time of crisis they wavered. Who should they obey?

'Come on Mum,' implored Mark, tugging at her arm. But she still resisted. Mark was torn between staying with her or going with his Dad.

Katie darted towards her father and took his hand. She was eager to get started on this great adventure. She had

115

implicit faith in her father. If he said they had to go then she was not going to be left behind.

Mark thought to himself philosophically, 'If they really get to another planet they could always come back for us later on.'

'Don't worry, Mark,' said Mary confidently now, 'they'll be back in an hour or two, you'll see. I've seen enough of your father's crazy schemes.'

'You're the one that's crazy,' said Gruber and led the way to the front door. The others looked at Mary sympathetically but followed Gruber all the same.

'You're silly,' Katie shouted as she danced down the path.

'Katie,' choked Mary. Then again she thought to herself, 'What am I worrying about, they'll be back soon.'

Nora pressed her hand. 'Won't you change your mind? Come with us.'

Mary backed away, 'No. . . no. . .'

'Bye, Mark,' said Robert. 'I wish you were coming.'

If they hadn't needed him he would have stayed behind with his friend. Mark couldn't speak, and a tear rolled down his cheek. He stood with his mother, framed in the doorway, as the others waved and walked off into the darkness towards Berry Hill.

26

Let's get a move on,' said Benson.

'We seem to have been going in the wrong direction,' added Campbell.

'Does anyone know the right direction?' asked Matthews.

Both he and Campbell were quite new to the district and were not sure of their whereabouts anyway.

'I reckon we should follow the railway line,' Benson pointed in the direction where the line went round and disappeared through a small gorge. 'If I remember rightly, this track should lead us to a small halt, Perryn I think it's called.'

'Oh yes, I remember,' said Matthews, 'and there's a track which winds up the hill.'

'Which should lead us to the plane.'

'Hooray,' cried Campbell, 'we're nearly there.'

'Yes,' said Benson in a positive tone, 'we'll make it,' and he started off along the track.

'Let's sing "I'll take the high road and you take the low road". . .' Campbell sang in a deep baritone.

'Asshole,' Matthews interrupted. 'D'you want someone to hear us?'

'Or something?' ventured Benson uneasily.

They all stopped. 'What d'you mean, something?' asked Campbell.

'Spooks?' volunteered Matthews.

'No, it was that Marsden fellow. He was muttering something about dinosaurs,' replied Benson.

'Surely you don't believe that crap?' said Campbell incredulously.

'Jesus wept,' Matthews remarked impiously.

They looked at each other in consternation. 'I expect he was just delirious after his ordeal,' placated Benson, wishing he had not mentioned it. He realised he should not wind these two up, Matthews especially, who seemed the most superstitious.

'Yes,' agreed Campbell, 'let's keep our imaginations on what we are about to do. . .'

'And may the Lord make us truly thankful,' added Matthews.

They plodded on and soon came to the Halt. There was no station – just two platforms and a rickety sign on which the name of Perryn was barely visible. They sat down to get their breath. Campbell was still carrying his sack of viands. He untied it and brought out a box of meal pills.

'Here, have one of these,' and he shook them out and handed one each to Benson and Campbell. They chewed their pills dutifully.

'That should keep us going for a few more hours,' said Campbell. 'We need some strength to climb that hill.' There was just a few yards of flat stony ground and then the land rose steeply, with intermittent trees and bushes. It had once been a very attractive beauty spot.

'Well, we can't hang around to admire the scenery,' said Benson, 'not that you can see much in this light.'

He stood up and made for the hill. The other two followed and they started their trek up the winding path. They had not gone far when Matthews stopped. 'What's that noise?'

'Probably the students on the rampage,' said Benson in a matter of fact tone.

'Poor buggers, they know they're on the scent of something,' added Campbell.

'Talking of scent,' Matthews sniffed the turgid night air, 'there's a very weird smell around here.'

'Everything smells rotten now,' replied Benson soothingly. 'Come on or we'll never get there.'

No sooner had they resumed their climb than Campbell pointed, his eyes bulging, 'Look!'

They followed his shaking finger and saw a pair of eyes staring through a gap between two trees and a terrible stench wafted towards them.

'Bloody Hell,' quaked Matthews.

They stood as if frozen to the spot, then fear gave them the adrenalin they needed and their feet hardly touched the ground. After a while they paused, puffing and blowing with exertion. They looked back and could just see the outline of several large beasts stomping through the trees.

'Lucky they're going down,' whispered Campbell.

'I hope Gruber won't meet them,' said Benson fearfully.

'If they keep going that way they'll mow down the college,' added Matthews.

'And the students.'

'Poor sods,' said Benson.

They turned and ploughed on until they came to the top of the hill and there, only a short distance away, was the plane. They leapt forward with renewed vigour. 'There's someone there already,' exclaimed Campbell.

'Gruber,' shouted Benson, 'Gruber. . .'

27

Vikki, Philip and Ben scrambled onto the plane and sank into the seats, absolutely exhausted. 'Thank God we've got here,' said Philip.

'Not much good if the others don't make it,' added Don. He felt too anxious to get into the plane. He stood by the door and looked about warily.

'They'll make it,' Vikki called out in a confident tone. 'You'll see.'

'I hope you're right,' said Don.

Ben kept quiet and closed his eyes. Maybe he should have stayed down on the farm instead of getting mixed up in this schemozzle. He could have just faded out quietly. It seemed to him that he was either going to be trampled by dinosaurs or go up in the air with a bang. 'What a choice,' he thought.

Philip, who had very keen hearing, suddenly perked up. 'Hark, I hear noises abroad.' He tried to cheer them up.

Vikki went white. 'Not those dinosaurs again,' she cowered in her seat.

Then Don let out a yell, 'Nora!'

Suddenly everybody had converged – Campbell, Matthews and Benson from one side of the hill, and Gruber, Nora, Robert and Katie from the other. There was general confusion, crying and reunions. 'Oh, Don,' cried Nora as she fell into his arms and tears streamed down her face.

'I'm sorry, so sorry,' Don murmured as he stroked her hair.

He reached out and put his arm round Robert. 'Thank God you're both safe.'

Vikki leapt out of the plane and ran towards Campbell. Matthews stood back, realising he only took second place when it came to the nitty-gritty. He looked away. He couldn't stand any more of these reunions.

Benson and Gruber shook hands roughly. 'Here, take it,' said Gruber as he handed Benson the case. 'Let's get into the plane and see if we can get it fixed up.'

'Right,' said Benson, 'there's no time to lose.'

'Come on Robert,' Katie called, 'I want to sit in the front,' and she clambered into the plane.

Gruber turned and grabbed her. 'Oh no you don't, young lady, you'll sit where you're told,' and he hauled her to the ground.

'Benson and I will sit in the front. The adults will get in first. . .'

'Just like Noah's Ark,' murmered Matthews.

'How many of us are there?' queried Campbell.

'I make it eleven,' said Matthews.

So they piled into the plane. Ben and Philip at the back, then Don and Nora, Campbell and Vikki. 'You can sit on my lap,' said Campbell to Vikki.

'Come on Katie,' said Philip, 'here, sit with us.'

When they were packed in Gruber and Benson got in. 'What about you, Matthews? Robert must be near us. . .'

'I reckon we could still squeeze in another little one,' said Matthews.

'Hurry up and close the damn door,' yelled Gruber.

Benson was trying to open the case. 'I think we'll just have to put this on the floor.'

Matthews was about to get in when he saw two young children not more than ten years old. They had been watching for some time, but were afraid to be seen. Then Matthews saw that the boy was half blind and the girl was limping, with one leg shorter than the other. They were thin, dirty and dishevelled.

'We can't take cripples,' Gruber called out.

'Have some compassion, man,' answered Matthews. 'Come on kids, hop aboard.'

He stood by the plane like a guardian angel opening the gates to the next world. They limped towards him. Someone was at last being kind to them. They had been living rough for a long time, having been the survivors from a school for handicapped children. Matthews lifted first the girl and then the boy into the plane. 'It's going to be a bit of a squeeze.'

Ben called out, 'Here, let me get out and make room, I don't need to go.'

'For God's sake stop messing about. Get in Matthews,' Gruber shouted impatiently.

'We've got about four minutes,' called Benson.

Matthews then had a quick count. 'Oh my God, thirteen!' he said fearfully. He looked around to see if by any chance there might be another child lurking in the bushes.

Apart from Matthews they all remained quiet and subdued. They did not know that panic was mounting in the cockpit. Benson had opened the case. 'There's nothing to fix the damn plug into,' he said frantically.

'Tear the plug off then,' Gruber barked. 'Push the wires straight into the electric circuit.'

'The Professor!' exclaimed Benson. 'Where is he?'

'I thought he was with you,' said Gruber crossly. In fact he had completely forgotten about the Professor. He had merely assumed that he was with Benson and the others. Anyway, it was too late now. He called through the door of the cockpit. 'It's nearly countdown, haven't you shut the door yet?'

'O.K.' Matthews climbed into the plane and then turned round. He could just make out the figure of a girl panting up the hill. In the distance was the sound of human voices which seemed to be getting closer. 'Come on,' shouted Matthews, 'just room for one more.'

He caught hold of her arms as she was about to collapse and hauled her into the plane. The door slammed shut. 'Shhh. . . quiet,' roared Gruber. 'Robert, get ready.'

Campbell also was thinking of the Professor. 'I expect he stayed behind deliberately to give the younger people a chance. We owe all this to him, that is if it works. Here we are, packed into this little plane like a can of sardines, expecting a miracle to happen with a bit of music and a tomato shape.'

Matthews looked out of the window and saw students pounding towards the plane. Adam was beating on the door shouting, 'Let me in.' Matthews opened the door and put a boot into Adam's face which sent him reeling, and quickly closed the door again. Luckily the others were some way behind. 'Just in time,' he breathed.

The children were open-mouthed at this great adventure. The boy who was half blind thought perhaps he had died and was being taken to the next world by all these kind people. Even Katie, who had such faith in her father, began to wonder if this was just acting out a fairy tale.

They all had their own thoughts, some thinking of the past and some wondering if nothing was going to happen at all and they would just go trooping home again.

Then, as the tremulous notes of the harp rippled through the air, the plane itself seemed to take on a different configuration, as if the metal was expanding and contracting ready to dissolve into particles.

Robert crouched just behind Benson and Gruber, getting ready to emit the final note which, for some obscure reason on the Professor's part, had to be live and could not be registered on the tape.

As the music became louder they all held their breath, completely spellbound, and as Robert emitted the last treble note the plane began to vibrate faster and faster – there was a blinding flash of light and all that was left was an outline of white dots etched against the sky in the shape of a brain, or was it a tomato?

28

Mark was looking out of the window, although it was dark. 'Perhaps they will come back,' he thought. Then, all of a sudden the sky was lit up. 'Mum,' he shouted, 'it looks like fireworks!'

Mary rushed to the window and then to the front door. They both went outside and saw the aftermath of the holocaust with the dinosaurs.

'What on earth is it and what's all that noise?' asked Mary in a perplexed tone.

Gradually the sparks and the noise died down. 'Look, the Professor's come back,' shouted Mark joyfully, glad that he was not the only one to stay behind. The Professor crept down the path looking very old and tired. Mary took his arm and led him indoors.

'Come in and have a nice sit down. Perhaps we could watch a film.'

'I haven't seen a film for years,' said the Professor, sinking into a chair with a sigh.

Mark switched on the video and his mother and the Professor settled down cosily to watch it, but he could not concentrate. All manner of thoughts were running through his head. He looked at his mother and for two pins would have run out of the house and up the hill to join his Dad in this wild adventure. He suddenly felt as old as the Professor. 'It's no good, it's too late now.'

'Why doesn't the video come on?' said Mary querulously.

'It's as dead as a dodo,' answered Mark. 'Listen!' He jumped up and ran out into the garden.

Mary got up and helped the Professor to his feet. 'We'd better go and see what it is,' she sighed.

Outside they could hear a beautiful sound. It was like the ripple of the waves, the sigh of wind in the trees, the trilling of birds and then a noise like the thunder of a volcano. The ground shook under their feet and they heard a faint, 'Whoooshhh', and then silence.

And in the sky they saw the outline of bright dots. 'What's that?' asked Mark.

'It's the shape of the brain,' replied the Professor.

'It looks more like a tomato to me,' said Mark.

'It worked,' cried the Professor.

'Ohhh. . .' Mary burst into tears, sobbing hysterically.

'Never mind, Mum,' said Mark soothingly, 'they'll come back for us, you'll see.'

He put an arm round each of them and led them back into the house.